Praise for *One Day I'll Tell You Everything*

'*One Day I'll Tell You Everything* is a sumptuous read. My senses were set alight—I could feel the sun, smell the air, taste the snow. At its heart lies the story of Adèle—a woman who is at once fleeing, and reconciling with, her past. It is Adèle who gives this novel its pulse. Every page thrums with her love.' Melanie Cheng, author of *Room for a Stranger*

'A superb novel, both thrilling and consoling.' *Le Soir*

'In *One Day I'll Tell You Everything*, Emmanuelle Pagano infiltrates the intricacies of families and romantic turmoil; she strips bare the eternal duel between absolute love and failure to understand… Pagano writes with sensitivity, from the bottom of her heart. She takes us into a love story that is as troubling as it is exhilarating. Whether she's writing about bodies in torment or her Ardèche mountains, her writing is all sensuality.' *Télérama*

'Close to being a masterpiece. A novel full of grace that takes us into the heart of female experience…There is something luminous and gentle about Emmanuelle Pagano's prose…We do not expect the female narrator to have been a him. The theme of femininity carried by the substance of the writing itself takes on a deeper and

more radical meaning…Pagano also excels at rendering palpable the lives of a tight-lipped, enclosed community, where the wind is a hazard and where farm anecdotes can become local mythology.' *Le Matricule des anges*

'*One Day I'll Tell You Everything* is a novel to be savoured, that one wants to protect like a secret garden. Emmanuelle Pagano invites us on a journey, at the heart of which is a feminine identity discovering itself, coming to life before our eyes.' *360 degrees*

'To live in one's body as if it were a foreign, inhospitable land: this thread of suffering runs through the novel like a burn…Pagano is also a screenwriter and has a talent for creating images…A vibrant, fundamental truth emerges from these pages.' *Le Temps*

'This novel is above all moving because of the author's extraordinarily beautiful language—both harsh and uncompromising like the climate, and exquisitely crafted and poetic—when, for instance, Adèle describes herself as masculine or feminine, depending on whether it is before or after her operation.' *Quotidien national*

'Adèle's brother has never understood her, and hasn't spoken to her for ten years…Apart from her brother, no one in the village knows the truth about Adèle, not even Tony, with whom she is having a love affair she never thought possible...The truth emerges from the mouth of a child, one of the adolescents Adèle drives to and from school every day, and who constitute as many mirrors in which she does and doesn't recognise herself...The vulnerabilities of this person living in a body that is alien to her are subtly echoed by the issues of identity experienced by her adolescent passengers. Emmanuelle Pagano's voice is understated and brilliant; she reveals the convulsions of the soul, the subtle feelings of her characters—*One Day I'll Tell You Everything* is a heartrending book.' *Tageblatt*

'A writer of immense originality: she has a sharp awareness of bodies and the visible or secret movements of those bodies, a language rich with images, seemingly familiar, but in reality shrewdly sophisticated, and a deep knowledge of nature and all the forces that pass through nature.' *Le Pays d'Auge*

'Pagano writes about siblings, about love and lies, about life slipping away, and about adolescents who are full of life. She speaks about bodies transforming, seasons changing, and memories that never fade. This extraordinarily beautiful novel, both sensitive and thoughtful, has an astute and deeply affecting ending.' *Livre et Lire*

Emmanuelle Pagano was born in 1969 and lives in the Ardèche in south-east France. She has written fifteen novels; *One Day I'll Tell You Everything* won the European Prize for Literature and has been translated into more than fifteen languages. Emmanuelle regularly collaborates with artists working in other disciplines. emmanuellepagano.wordpress.com

Penny Hueston has translated books by Marie Darrieussecq, Patrick Modiano and Raphaël Jerusalmy, among others.

One Day I'll Tell You Everything

Emmanuelle Pagano

Translated from the French by Penny Hueston

t

TEXT PUBLISHING MELBOURNE AUSTRALIA

textpublishing.com.au

The Text Publishing Company
Swann House, 22 William Street, Melbourne Victoria 3000, Australia

The Text Publishing Company (UK) Ltd
130 Wood Street, London EC2V 6DL, United Kingdom

Originally published in France under the title *Les Adolescents troglodytes* by
P.O.L. Éditeur, Paris, 2007
Published by The Text Publishing Company, 2020

Book design by Jessica Horrocks
Cover photo by Bo Bo/Stocksy
Typeset in Granjon 13.75/19.5 by J&M Typesetting

Printed and bound in Australia by Griffin Press, part of Ovato, an accredited
ISO/NZS 14001:2004 Environmental Management System printer.

ISBN: 9781922268914 (paperback)
ISBN: 9781925923407 (ebook)

A catalogue record for this book is available from the National Library
of Australia.

I walk in the footprints
left by my brother until
we reach the bus stop.

Lola, winter, 2004–05

Thursday,
1st September

(my break)

As usual I was soon sick of the fair, the commotion. I sneaked away, down the back road with the wind turbines, then along a path to the right, into the forest. I squatted for a pee in the sweet-smelling humus, and sat down on a cool, flat stone to rest.

Behind me, in the distance, I could hear the bass throb of the fair. Bending over gave me a slight headache, which did me a world of good. I scratched the moist earth and found a cracked acorn that was a bit rotten. I put it in my pocket, then rubbed my hands together. But there was not much point in wiping the dirt off my hands, because I felt peculiar as I stood up, and the whole time I was walking I clutched, almost crushed, that rotten half-acorn in my clammy palm.

I know why I felt peculiar: it's because there was something about the fair that made me think of the start of the school year. With the change of wind, I could still hear the sound of the clay-pigeon shooting, even in the depths of the forest. And nasty big fluorescent-green flies, also carried by the wind, swarmed on the back of my neck.

I kept walking, more and more irritated. It was stifling in the clearings and my cheeks felt unpleasantly hot. But in the forest, in the shadows that were still purplish from the rampant columbine flowers, I had the persistent sensation of being almost too cold. There is no mean temperature on the plateau, no springtime, only deviations. It's hot, and then it's not; it's summer, but it's winter. Back to school already.

I know perfectly well today's the day, but two weeks ago, during the Pansy Flower Fete, that wind and the racket from the fair turned my mind back to my kids again, and I didn't want to think about them then, no, not yet.

~

It was just this morning that my affection for them returned, as it does every year, when I get up early, with a lot of time to spare, collect the bus from the garage, calmly get myself ready, and cruise through the early dawn, before picking them up, one by one, or almost, at the start of their first day of school.

Near the lake there is a median strip where I can park. Next to an apple tree. The rotten apples on the ground roll underneath the bus and stick to the wheels, all squashed and mushy. I climb out and pick up two that are perfectly ripe. The day is beginning; I can scarcely see a thing. I'll have to leave soon, but I have time now. From my spot up here, you can't see the water, but you can see the lake, see clearly that the trees are there below the surface, in the sinkhole in the middle. Early in the mornings, that empty space is full of mist. It's the hole in the lake, the lake, my break, my sea, my time.

I often take this break on my commute, before I start, or at the end.

Even though the apples don't know it, it's not really autumn, we're only at the beginning of September, daybreak is still early, but the start of school makes the leaves fall, anyone can see that, and my shoes are all damp with dew at this parking spot above the forest that surrounds the lake.

Soon daybreak will come later, and I will only see my kids while it is still dark.

I approach the trees lower down, closer to the sink-hole's spindrift shadows. I take the path, this bit of track that I have forged myself, by dint of heading down here patiently, or helter-skelter, nervous, wanting to get there fast, pushing through the trees and the frost. It descends almost impercep-tibly, with branches that scrape, patches of wet chill, water smells, and on some days the far-off sound of beavers, like on the river when I was little. Scratching noises that scuttle away from my foot-steps, from my memory.

At the end of my path there is a weeping birch tree, tall, old, bent, and beneath it my shelter, oval, narrow but comfortable. I sit down. But, despite the calmness within me, despite the seclusion I share with it, the lake is noisy, dribbling cold between the roots, all grey and black.

This lake is never calm, it is a deaf volcanic crater, blind as well, a grey hole, the sound of its backwash a thousand years old. The less the lake sees, the less we see, the more thunderous its echo.

The artificial lake on the bottom farm is so much quieter.

At the base of my birch tree the lake continues its noise, a constant noise that often envelops me before I arrive here. It guides me in the first glimmer of morning. A low, full sound, as if the volcano were no longer extinct.

When I was a little boy, I would often pretend to be dead. I wanted people to weep over me. I wept for myself, usually near a tree, under it or up inside it, just like I'm crying today, a woman weeping, in my weeping birch tree, hidden by the slender branches.

Here I am, eating one of the apples, a woman sitting in my female tree, its hips full of water.

I say that, but I've never looked. I've never picked a birch flower and opened it up to find out, and I'm not alone there—I really wonder who takes an interest in the sex of trees. I actually think the birch tree, unlike the willow tree, has two sexes: the female flowers are above, on the higher branches. I look up, but I can't see anything; it's not the right time, or the right season. All I can see is a deluge of drab branches; all I can see is whiteness that is almost blue, a dirty pale blue that has been immersed in the peat bog. My tree is more weeping, more bent and trailing than a willow.

I part the twigs that prevent me from seeing the silt at my feet. In a flash, the tree and I are blanketed by a surge of water that swiftly turns into rolling waves. The lake absorbs all the light, reflects nothing, neither face nor gaze, neither sunlight nor haze.

I toss my apple core, and I cannot see, cannot even guess where it falls. My birch is blue like all the trees around the lake. Scarcely any orange, even in autumn, because of the dominant, towering presence of the conifers, and scarcely any green in summer either, because of the grey, almost black, gaping hole of the volcano, filled with sinkhole slosh. In winter, there is no visibility, or very little. This is my murky blue space. The trees are not altered by the seasons, and time and water erosion have barely knotted their bark even after decades. My birch, like the rest of them, is blue, covered in dirty bruises; leafless in winter, it takes on the blue marine of the spruce trees; ageless, it takes on the shape of water, of tears, straightens itself a little, then, with its glabrous, soft leaves, it lets itself be lapped by ultramarine mosses. But the lake only spills back into itself, and my birch bathes in the same spot in the lake's water, in the lake's air, and I am sitting beneath it. Snug. My break.

I stay here now because I need the lake and the shade in order to remember, to snivel over my memories like an old woman. Memory has to be washed and refilled every day.

When I was a little boy, I used to hide, I looked for places like this, where I could sort out my feelings, and my mother would call out my name, right near me, without seeing me: her voice blaring before it faded, then came back, faded again, and ended up far enough away for me to be able to start thinking.

In the forest, years ago, over the sound of my mother's voice, I heard a bell right next to my hiding spot. I wondered what the hell that cow was doing there, so far from the main fields. I parted the bushes and looked around a bit. But I was looking up too high. Suddenly I saw her, lying down, the crushing mass of her, wallowing in the soft, damp leaves, and it made me sick to see those leaves coming out of there, out of that enormous body in a heap on the earth all swollen with water. But the cow was more distressed than I was. She wasn't one of ours, nor the neighbours'; she wasn't one of the cows I knew, and I really knew a lot, dozens of them. This one was white, dirty and panting, overcome with cramps, bellowing. She wanted to get up because I was there, but I knew how to calm her down by placing my hand next to the painful area, pressing just enough. The outstretched legs of the calf were sticking out, stuck there. The skin of the torn sack hung empty. Too late. But I pulled like a deaf person (deaf to my mother's still audible voice), with all the strength of

11

my eight or nine years or whatever I was, to help her expel her dead calf. It was enormous, and heavy, too big, a calf with sturdy hips, a calf for the agricultural show. My arms were slippery with blood and mud, and soggy dead leaves. I didn't manage to get it out. I wanted to go and tell someone, but I didn't; I wasn't sure if I'd done the right thing. I didn't tell anyone; I heard my mother's voice again calling my name and I was scared she'd get cross with me. I headed slowly back to the farm, trying to diffuse the emotion that was making my whole body writhe and shiver. I could have borrowed the calf-puller, but I didn't know how to use it or carry the huge thing, bigger than me: there was no way. I kept thinking; I dragged my feet.

My mother seemed annoyed because my clothes were dirty from the forest. She knelt down and said, I'm not going to get cross with you, I'm happy when you play in the forest, but please be careful, I won't be able to find a way to dry the washing in this weather.

For my mother, the weather meant the drizzle, the mist, the usual dampness around there, on the bottom farm, the rain, the fog or the snow, or even rain, fog and snow mixed together by the wind, the fog made of fresh snow because of the snowstorm, but this weather also meant all the time it took to do the laundry, the housework and everything else. She kept telling us, you don't know how long it takes, and it's already milking time, your father needs help in the cowshed, Axel, and you, come and help me with the basket, please.

I took one handle of the basket, my mother the other, and we climbed up to the hayloft.

No one ever spoke about the cow that came to calve, and died, rotting in the forest near our place. I know how quickly big animals like that start to stink, but no one said a thing. Neither did I.

Perhaps I dreamt it up, to invent an excuse for myself, to explain my filthy clothes, my distress, an explanation for me alone.

I wonder whether the artificial lake, by covering up my childhood, brought up these bodies, or what was left of them. For me, what's left is the memory of all that effort of blood and of mud, of the dead leaves I rubbed myself with and blew my nose on afterwards, sobbing.

I cried a lot when I was little, often, and I didn't know why.

After my operation, it was the same thing: I dissolved into tears when the first thing I felt on waking up was a pain so strong that it flooded from my new, raw vagina all the way into my mother's womb. I was woozy from the morphine and contemplating my memories from all angles. There I was, carrying the heavy body of the dead calf all by myself. I opened my eyes again. And there was the ever-so-light foetus, so slight in my terrified little boy's hands, terrified by this minuscule, unfinished baby, by all the blood coming out, and the swashing pools of it still to come out, by the screams of my father, who was telling me, let go of it, as he was leaning with all his weight on my mother's pelvis, trying stupidly to stop the haemorrhaging. She had already given up: she was emptied out. We lived too far from the hospital, and my mother had said to my brother, who wanted to call the firefighters, leave it, you know I've had experience with this, it's not the first time, anyway the snow is too heavy.

In pain, and under morphine that could scarcely relieve it, I saw the two little bodies, the big calf and my little brother—my little purple foetus—swimming, alive, in the waters of the lake. The oversized calf went under. It was as if the scrap of flesh, my little brother, my little sister, was being cradled by underwater movements. It floated up. In my delirium, I reached out my hand, I touched a raised arm, a slender, bluish leg, both floating on the surface, a slight shoulder, hollowed out like a piece of driftwood.

I would never have a child, that's what my brother kept saying: If you do that, you'll never have a child. I had just done that, yes, and too bad, it was all well and good if I never had dead babies.

The different blues of the water are not the same as the blues of the trees, but in the shade of the lake they are impossible to differentiate.

(on the way to the high school)

I'm driving towards the teenagers, their shadows.
They must be shivering a bit this first morning back.

I pick up the two who live furthest away first. They
are odd boys, friends and yet separate. They never sit
next to each other, and yet they're always together.
   The first one on my run, the one who gets up
earliest, is the eldest of three children with big gaps
in their ages. The family is indifferent to the local
gossip surrounding them. They say around here that
the mother is a witch because, instead of discarding
nettles on the manure like old people do, she puts
them in everything, in soups, teas, decoctions, and
also because she has books all over the house, even
in the kitchen. Her oldest boy is called Sylvain.

His skin is soft (thanks to poultices for relieving acne), his eyes and complexion dark brown, like the forest. Then comes Lise, pale, translucid, and a much younger brother, Minuit, two and a half years old, tiny next to his schoolbag, golden-blond all over, even his skin. He wriggles around so much that it's a wonder he ever sleeps (I still haven't found the off button, Lise confided one evening, sighing).

When they told me, four years ago, about the dispensation for under-fives in the shuttle bus, I feared the worst. Disciplining toddlers, settling them. Finding booster seats. Buckling their seatbelts, wiping their noses, their cheeks, don't cry, that's enough, come on, that's enough. But there were no horrible snotty-nosed kids. For a long time I only picked up older kids, and then after Easter last year two very young boys, but there has never been a problem.

Minuit is always with his sister; he holds on to her as if he were some kind of appendage, and Lise's whole body is in tune with her brother's. When they climb in, pressed together, bumping against each other, they look like a gleaming, coppery two-headed monster. Minuit flanks her, squeezed against her hip, and Lise pulls his little face to her belly in an older girl's maternal gesture. I don't know how you say a big sister's gesture: fraternal doesn't work, and maternal only just works, but not quite. I envy her those gestures, those postures, that warm mouth, still dribbling, against her jumper. My little brother would never have let me do that; my brother says that he has never had a sister, that he will never have one.

Minuit will have grown a bit since June; perhaps Lise will be able to sit down and unlatch him from her body.

This golden-haired youngest brother is so beautiful (and has long hair and an androgynous first name), but no one thinks Minuit is a girl. He's definitely a boy, with the whole kit and caboodle: a boisterous manner, brusque gestures, square shoulders. After the Easter school holidays, he was still tiny beneath his mop of hair. He was like a lion—no, a tigger (already less frightened after a few weeks, but still clinging to his sister). Oh, sorry, *tiger*.

The other little boy is Hugues, who is almost three now, and who was already behaving just like a big kid last year. He's a little peasant boy, like I was, or rather like my little brother was, sturdy and smart.

The teenagers set up the booster seats before getting off at school. If he has to remind the others, Sylvain does it in a voice that leaves no room for argument:

The seats for the little kids, hey, are you guys deaf, we have to get out the kids' seats.

One morning he told me he had other younger brothers:

But they live in Germany, and I have more, too, older brothers, but they're creeps. On the other hand, he said, smiling, I only have one sister. And you, Adèle, are you someone's sister?

Then he slouched into his hoodie, without waiting for the response that I wouldn't have given him anyway.

He lives with his mother and the two youngest boys on the other side of the mountain. I've only seen the mother once. She could be a witch; she's certainly a recluse, greeting you as if it hurts her chapped lips to speak. She's no chatterbox. I don't like talking much either, but I'm not rude. Her face reminds me of something; I don't know what, since she never speaks.

The second boy on my route lives on this side of the mountain; he gets on when I've driven back around. Because they make me do this circuit around the mountain, where the Loire River has its source, I call them Loire kids, Ligerians, I even say my Loire kids, my Ligerians. I should call them Upper Loire kids, Upper Ligerians, but it's a mouthful, and as I only call them that in my head, it's my business.

My second Ligerian has the name of a flower, I think. I think Niel is the name of a flower. Nielle, he says—he often has to correct me, as does Sylvain and the others who copy Sylvain: Nielle des Blés, corncockle flower, but it doesn't grow above one thousand metres, that's why he's so small, so skinny, says Sylvain. Nielle never replies; he doesn't even seem upset.

Nielle and Sylvain, like a lot of former townies, have eco-parents, bush types, rough as guts. The other kids make fun of them in a more or less amiable way. Their pants are suitably stained.

~

Oh yeah, former townies, I dunno (Sylvain gets a bit annoyed sometimes). I've always lived in the sticks, my mother has too. But it wasn't strictly local, so for you guys that's far away, just because it's not right here. The others counter: Adèle, no one says that about you, you've been here a long time, it's not the same, and anyway you know everyone, even the old people, so that means it's okay to say you've always been here. Honestly, whichever old person we talk about, you know them, even the dead ones. Is it because you've got an old lady's first name?

Before they run out of taunts, the boys put me at ease by insulting me, and laughing. They're often two-faced like that: smiling or even sharing secrets when they're by themselves, then sometimes going too far when they're in a group.

The kids repeating a year have a chip on their shoulder. Sylvain cops it for being a smartarse jerk, a maverick in a hoodie.

Just because my mother has three thousand books instead of three cheap paperbacks you can wipe your bum with doesn't mean she's not from the country.

Oh yeah, books of spells, recipe books to turn you into a toad. But you're already a toad.

Sometimes they stop there; sometimes they stand up, argue and scuffle, but not Nielle. When there's a tussle, I brake and pull over. They know they have to be quiet and sit down if they want me to start the engine again.

They've never taken advantage of it to be late for school.

If Sylvain has stood up, he sits back down in his seat at the other end of the bus from Nielle. They stare at each other.

They have a close and tempestuous friendship, which has not changed in four years, not since their first year of high school, when their families arrived, almost simultaneously, on the plateau. They are joined at the hip and yet loners, silent when they're together, sometimes bound by a complicity that nothing could undermine. Nielle and Sylvain, my Loire kids, my Ligerians. Two big boys, both the oldest of single-parent families. (In the beginning, tongues were wagging about the witch, but she didn't let them push her around, or, rather, she just let them gossip.) Nielle's father is a widower, so, respect.

Nielle says, Hello, Adèle, welcome back, and he goes and sits away from Sylvain, flicking Sylvain's hood down as he passes. I'm happy nothing has changed.

The bus that has been my life for ten years is a small van, a four-wheel drive with sliding doors, nine seats. This is the first year all the seats are filled. Eight children, eight teenagers, morning and evening.

Sometimes the route changes in winter, when we have to detour round the snowdrifts. The commute with the big kids is not quite the same as the commute with the little kids. Even if a lot of the big kids have younger brothers and sisters, some of the big kids are still the youngest in their family. And some of the little kids are the oldest in their family, but you can be certain that none of those children will be an only child. I don't know any only children around here, even among the in-law additions to a family.

~

When I was a little boy, there was one, but her parents had her very late, that's why. She smelled bad.

I have to pick up the youngest and oldest children of the new families from other hamlets, other farms. My trip changes every time there's a new fraternal regrouping.

No fights today. It's normal on the first day back at school.

Joël is smiling, looking good, all dressed up; that's not like him at all. Julien gets on a bit further down the road, the fourth pick-up on my trip (and, like Joël, starting Year Nine). He whistles when he sees Joël, shakes his hand and sits down, then gets up straightaway (jostling Sylvain):

Adèle, you too look splendid, but you always do.

It's his way of saying hello, gently ironic, awkwardly polite.

Nielle turns around and belatedly notices the transformation in Joël's appearance. He even seems to be more alert, but soon enough he returns to his separate space, the space he reserves for himself, right there, just behind that gaze of his, an angel in a daydream, enveloped by fantasies of girls, and by the girls' dreams and fantasies, because of his freckles, his delicate build, his parchment-white face beneath his colourless hair. During the first few days of his Year Seven, I thought Nielle was going to vomit when we took the corners, but he has that sickly look all the time. And the girls are maternal, they go up to him and ask how he is. But they'll never know: Nielle is a mystery that only Sylvain is allowed to get close to.

There she is, the first girl. She is also the first one to bring me, barely masked beneath a lemon-cinnamon synthetic fragrance, the lingering, benevolent odour of the stables. I inhale and I look at her. How she has changed. Over a single summer, teenage girls deviate: they don't become adults, they don't leave childhood either, but they deviate, uncannily, into an impossible age. How old could this one be? Anywhere from thirteen to fifteen, it's impossible to know, impossible to understand.

Nadège looks at me. I'd definitely say she was sixteen or seventeen if I didn't know that she's never skipped a year. She's in Year Ten, like Sylvain, Nielle and Sébastien. I've got a lot of big kids this year. She's smiling, not at me, not at the boys, she's smiling, but at no one, perhaps at someone who's not there. The four boys are silent. Sébastien gets in after Nadège. He's the fifth and final boy, the oldest. There are two more girls to pick up. It's easy to keep count. I'm always told in advance, at the stop beforehand, when there's one missing, because here everybody knows everything about everyone, except about Nielle, and Nielle is often absent.

I was also often absent in primary school and high school, but it was another time, another place—another place and yet the same; it was probably a whole other story.

Nadège turns around. Sébastien has nudged her. I look at Sébastien. He adores me, so he gives an apologetic gesture with his hands. Nadège sits down. I get going on the road again, and it's the road that gets me going again, just like every year.

~

There are a lot of twists and turns on the trip, but it's almost flat. It's horizontal—my thoughts rise from there and descend no further, or rather they descend, descend, and rise no further. The kids, even the young ones, tap me gently on the shoulder when I miss a stop, but that doesn't happen very often.

I'm thinking about the bewitcher, the mother of Sylvain, Lise and Minuit. No one knows what she lives off, or how she provides for her three children, or where the three fathers are. Despite the similarity between the two youngest, there are certainly three fathers, according to the rumour mill, which is never entirely wrong. Sylvain scowls inside his hoodie if anyone gets too nosy. Lise just shrugs and smiles. Her mother the witch, the wild one, her nose buried in her books.

Rumour has it, however, that she doesn't know how to write, that she scribbles indecipherable marks, that she muddles through with Sylvain's help when it comes to official documents. That's what the postman says, anyway, and also that she won't even offer you a coffee, not to mention a glass of wine, she stays there with her nose in her books, but she's pretending, for sure, there's no such thing as someone who knows how to read but not to write.

My brother used to make fun of me.

He called me the bookworm girl. I wasn't yet a girl in the eyes of other people, no, I scarcely was in my own eyes, but coming from my brother, it was especially insulting to be called a girl. Reading instead of playing football was a girly thing to do. The bookworm girl was as bad as the fibber girl, the girlfriend (the worst name of all), the bratty girl.

We used to argue all the time, and the rest of the time we fought, or rather he fought me, wrestling me to the ground until I begged him to stop because I couldn't move, and soon wouldn't have been able to breathe, that's for sure.

Afterwards, I didn't say a word. I didn't berate him at all. He should have called me the silent girl. Mostly I read in order not to speak.

As a little boy, until he was perhaps about five years old, he agreed to play tea parties with me, on condition that he could be Davy Crockett (Maman made us costumes). We dressed up in calfskin pants, the leather still rough, badly tanned and strong-smelling. We carried the saucepans, our rabbit-skin caps, all our bits and pieces, down to the riverbank, where I cooked up some grub using peat for fuel. It smelled good.

My brother grew faster than I did, and when I was nine or ten, he was stronger and taller than me (he was only about eight). He loved fighting, I didn't, and I became aware of my difference by seeing myself as a kind of inverse female figure in his ever more brutal games. I came to understand myself as a girl slowly, implicitly, through my body and through my big little brother's punches. He was Davy Crockett and I was everything else: the trees, the beavers, the solitude, the peat bog lapped by the river.

The river no longer exists, it's a lake now—artificial, wide and flat, lying immense and still over the top of our farm. Our farm, our home, now a waterlogged phantom, a ruin, almost destroyed, reappears each time the lake is drained. And when the waters abate, the stables, the paths, and the river's bridges reappear.

~

Nadège gets up to come and sit next to me (move over Joël, and Joël obediently heads to the back of the bus), the boys are annoying her, and anyway she wants to tell me that she saw me briefly at the Pansy Flower Fete: But why didn't you stay, what's the point of coming if you don't stay for a while?

The irritating benefit of short trips in a bus is that two students sit up the front, on my right.

So you came to see someone, and then he wasn't there, or did you come because you'd been invited by someone, some friends, and then you were really bored out of your brain once you got there, is that it, Adèle? No way, I'm sure you went to see a guy, and he wasn't there. What's he like?

I smile. They're all used to my silence, I often reply with smiles, or not. Yes or no written on my face. Nadège is pleased to know that I'm in love, or something like that, well, something like that, right, Adèle?

Something like that, yes, but with a gap of a few years. When I was Nadège's age, I used to go to the village fetes with my brother. We went there to be seen, to flirt and drink. Well, he went to be seen, to flirt and drink. I followed him. I was the older brother, but I followed him, always. I stuck close to him, he called me his little barnacle, laughing about it, and despite everything I liked his laughter. He often made fun of me, and often in public, as if conspiring to provoke something, fate, my future. And now and then he would make fun of me to my face, just the two of us, in an odd kind of complicity. I liked it, our private jokes, and his laughter, as if he was suddenly okay with me after all: Of course, my little barnacle, why not, one day you'll be a girl, yes, you already are, come on, just in the body of a boy, tell that to Papa, you'll see. He guffawed and grabbed my shoulder to knock me off balance. I lost my balance, of course, and in the same movement my body seized on my brother's laughter. I toppled into his jibes, tempered as they were with well-hidden tenderness and intimacy.

He was the opposite, he always kept his balance, well, it was more like the balance that kept him. He climbed up anything, trees, rocks, cliffs, the barn

wall, he was not the slightest bit afraid of heights—
they gave him confidence.

Nadège stays close to me. I muster a meagre effort to
say yes or no to her. You know, I add, I just wanted
to see if it was still the same as when I was young.
So she's really happy now, thinking that as a young
girl I used to go out and get hit on. Then she goes
back to her seat.

Hit on: I can't stand that expression. I picture myself
being examined right to my inner core, a pole pene-
trating my bodily fluids, probed as if I was a corpse.

I stop to pick up the two little girls in Year Seven
(no Year Eights this year), girlfriends, neighbours,
almost sisters, who are never apart. Not friends like
my Loire kids, who are never together. No, these
two girls are like Siamese twins. And sometimes
furious with each other, which is part and parcel
of their relationship. Their names are Marine and
Marie, I kid you not. I've been driving them around
since they were in kindergarten. They're very

anxious about starting high school and when they get in the bus the others tease them. They sit up the front with me, next to each other, since Nadège has gone back with the boys (okay, okay, Adèle, I'm putting my seatbelt on, give me a second), and Joël is still there too. They both start talking at the same time to warn me that the gorges are shut. I tell them, I know, I'm going to go around via the saddle, don't worry, girls, that's why the timetable has changed. You know, Adèle, they say there's going to be a landslide. Hey, no, there's already been a landslide; no, there hasn't; yes, there has.

Off we go with a shouting match, finally, the first for the year, the Year Ten and Year Nine kids join in. Stories about rockfalls. Around here, it's like the White Lady stories, the woman in white on the side of the road. Everyone knows something and knows nothing. Everyone has seen some sort of rockfall, or their brother or their cousin has. On a bend in the road; no, it was where the white lines converge, that's where people have been killed; don't be so stupid. No one's died this time, there was a landslide this summer. No, there wasn't, not yet. Yes, there was. Oh, you're such an idiot, it was years ago. I calm them down by reassuring them that it's just reinforcement works on the cliff face, but it's a major construction site, it'll be there for a few months, so we'll be taking the detour for a long time. Until the snow season? Yes, until the snow, perhaps even until after the snow.

Seen from above, the gorges look quite strange. The weather has been cold, and all the humidity rising from the river turned into frost overnight, so it appears bleached in the dawn light. It's as if the frost is trapped in a demarcated area. It stops around the road level, overflowing on each side of the river without reaching the top of the rock face.

If we stared down into the whiteness, it could be dark grey when we look up, but once again the light shining in our eyes is bright and clear. It's our new school term, our countryside, in black and white and grey.

And that guy, Adèle, you know, that guy, do you think he'll be there this year? I look at Sébastien in the rear-vision mirror. He is the only student repeating for the second time, he remembers the first time we had to make a huge detour. I watch his eyes grow wide.

We had seen the guy after the first big landslide, more than five years ago. At the time, the firemen did mention someone dying in their car, but they never found the body, only bits of the wrecked car, weeks, months later, crumbled like mica into the surface of the rock. I had to drive a long way down below the plateau and head for several kilometres along a road that was three lanes wide and yet wedged against the mountains, all hairpin bends. About six o'clock in the evening, on the return run from school, on a bend, one precise bend, always the same, there was a man, his back against the crash barrier, perilously, facing the road, always around six o'clock and always in the same position. He was staring straight ahead, slightly to the left. We didn't have time to get a good look at him as we drove past, but because he was there every day, same time, same bend, we had the weird opportunity to look at him in bits, a different part of him every day, until we knew his unchanging items of clothing by heart, his age, uncertain but at least fifty, his idiotic position. His suicidal gaze hidden by a tatty balaclava.

No one on the plateau knew him. He must have been from down below, and come up at the end of the afternoon to sit it out against the crash barrier, waiting for whoever or whatever. In any case, we speculated about all sorts of things. From first thing in the morning, the stories came thick and fast. The young Year Seven kids (including Sébastien) were hoping he was the guy who had disappeared in the landslide. The older kids gave a plausible but ludicrous response: it was impossible because the cliff had collapsed right up the top, and we were right down the bottom (so how could he have got down?). Every morning, we'd be discussing why, how and especially whether he'd be there that evening. And every evening, when the students climbed in the bus, they didn't say a word until we reached that corner. Not saying a word meant whispering lots of things, but very softly, so as not to break the spell, the story, of our humdrum but extraordinary encounter.

One day the man was no longer there, but in the empty spot where he had been there was a distinct (Adèle, you're our witness) dent in the crash barrier. So then my teenagers got their parents involved.

They trawled through the news all weekend, as did I, and we called the hospitals down the mountain, the fire brigades at the top, but nothing matched up. One of the older kids decided then that he must have changed his timetable, and, oddly enough, that explanation was enough for us.

I silence the general excitement provoked by Sébastien's question. (What guy? What the hell's he talking about, Adèle?) No, we're not taking the same detour, we're not going that far down.

Aren't we taking the highway?

No, remember, we would've had to leave even earlier.

That's a pity.

And, anyway, you know very well there was just the dent in the rail, that's all.

Yeah, it's sad.

A few days ago, I made some enquiries about the construction site on the cliff face. This time the company that has landed the job is the one where my brother has found a temporary job. I walked over to the telephone, a book in my hand. I waited there for hours, I read several books, in fact, but my brother did not call me.

Last year, I was already keeping a close eye on the corbelling. I thought then that they needed reinforcing, for sure. I told the kids there was no way there'd be a landslide, and I was hopeful, but I feared the worst. I want to see my brother. If he's going to be here for a few months, he'll contact me.

My brother all alone above the ravines, for weeks, months, sleeping in a hut onsite. He would rather stay hanging up there, working on the mountain all by himself, than call his big sister. Joking without laughing with workmates he scarcely glimpses, all still roped together during lunch break. Stunned by the distinctive silence of thin air, by the noise of that solitude—of hundreds of metres of rocky escarpments above and below. His balance keeping him safe. I try to imagine him by remembering the letters he wrote me. He used to write to me a lot before my operation. I would illustrate his letters in my head, or sometimes on little pieces of paper.

I'd doodle a stick figure on the end of a rope: it was him.

Perhaps that's what she does, the witch? Illustrations, little storyboards based on tales she's read in her books. Perhaps they're tiny drawings that others think are just scribbles, or spells.

In my sketches, I never managed to portray the way my brother swung there, the movement of his arms and legs, nor his grimacing face.

I'm scared I'll forget his face. I haven't seen him for ten years. My brother all alone, like a fish up high there, quivering inside a steel creel, restless but safe, repairing an anti-submarine net, in order to secure the large, unstable fragments of rock above the roads, and to support the hundred-year-old corbelling. I think about the potential conflicts, about the averted military engagement implicit in these huge metallic bras on the mountain. Without giving it a second thought, my brother would install those anti-submarine nets that had been salvaged from the ocean after the cold war (and that's what he wrote to me, also without giving it a second thought). Now the nets are brand new, manufactured for peacetime landscaping. We still call them anti-submarine nets, but instead of being filled with deep water they overhang high-altitude roads that are almost aerial. Dynamic, high-impact ropes, with cable clamps, to subdue the mountain the way you'd hold back an insidious weapon of war that was advancing through the atmospheric waters. When the helicopter is not an option, the workers coil the ropes around their torso, so they can hoist themselves up high, thrown a little off

41

balance by the load. Lopsided men suspended up there.

They climb up and empty the nets regularly, getting rid of stones that have accumulated after storms. They change the nets every ten years. Yes, it's ten years since I've seen him.

My brother would make fun of me—if I could see him, and if we were still children. He would persist in sticking his face through the mesh of the netting until I was terrified. My brother, so proudly mercurial. Oh, she can drop dead, that stupid bitch, he must say to other people, without mentioning that I am his sister. My brother keeps quiet, but when he speaks he's always got it in for me. Only rarely does he talk about his big brother, when that was still what I was for him, the older brother. He has never had a sister and he never talks about other women, I'm sure of it, and anyway he wrote to me about it: Because of you, he said, knowing that you're going to do that, there's no way I can look at a chick without wanting to throw up.

My brother is a man whose feet are not on the ground, a man fixed in the air, he goes up and goes down, all roped up. When he's working, he flattens his body into the creases of the rocks, he forgets, his face is abraded by the elements, marked like the rock walls. He's a man with a plan, my brother, but a man without memory, no memory of me for ten years. A man who does not know himself or feel safe unless he is alone in the middle of nothing, resting with his expanded aerobic capacity, before launching himself into space once again, his arms loaded with motion sensors and tubing to install, and cables with which to attach the webbing. A man who is loaded up.

I remember him bringing in the wood with Papa: he pushed the door open with his shoulder, he threw the logs on the ground and Maman grumbled while I ran off to get a broom. He would smile, twigs on his jumper, which he brushed off as he watched me (and as he put his finger to his lips in complicity). I swept the twigs towards me.

The local council has issued a categorical order: there are to be no vehicles in the gorges until further notice, despite them being open on weekends and for tourists. (When I was a little boy we used to call them summer holidaymakers, even in winter.)

If I want to go there, it won't be in the bus. I won't be able to pretend I have to go there for the school run.

If I want to go there, it will most likely be specifically to see my brother.

(on the way to the primary school)

Lise gets in, and in the rear-vision mirror I notice immediately how much she too has changed. She settles Minuit in his seat, he's still tiny, golden-tinged, fidgety, but slightly less clingy. She fastens her little brother's seatbelt with gestures I haven't seen her use before, gestures I know so well. That curving of the right arm in order to avoid budding breasts— when I was a very young boy, I figured that out from girls who were older than I was. I copied it straightaway, and my brother noticed.

Instead of making fun of me he took me aside, concerned—he was only eight or nine, he didn't really understand—he just said, but why are you doing that? I lied and said I wasn't doing anything, leave me alone. Yeah, right, why don't you do things

45

normally, yeah, so you hurt your arm, say it, tell me. Axel, it's not there, it's my torso that hurts, the pain goes all the way to my shoulder, that's why I do it. I had started to say torso instead of chest.

Lise hasn't said hello to me.

She sits down and I keep driving.

The primary-school kids are very different from the high-school kids; even the Year Six students are a world apart from the Year Sevens, or from the kids repeating a year. So many things are different. The change of educational institution, family and friends, other students, the peer group, the teachers, the classroom assistants, the attitude of the parents, the physical changes that make your head spin, the particular gestures girls make with their arms. And for me driving them, there is the difference between the day and the night, especially in autumn.

The younger kids don't get to experience a night-time drive. They see a darkish dawn for a few minutes in November and December, but that's all. By the time we reach school, it's daytime for them, or almost. The older kids, on the other hand, have those two months of pick-ups entirely in darkness, and they scarcely see daylight from October to January.

But whether they're picked up or returned home by day or by night, whether they're children off to bed early, or adolescents shaken awake from a deep sleep by the demands of the pick-up, of high school, of the adults, there are daytime kids and night-time kids. Those who have their eyes open when they say hello, boisterous in the mornings and in the mists. Those who mutter morosely, exhausted when they say goodbye, and who are quick to bundle their bad tempers under their hoodies so they can make their black moods blacker. What I like most is not the wondrous and lively laughter of the little kids, laughter embellished with snowflakes, metallic and tinkling, no, I like the moods of my big kids: obnoxious, crude, filthy and so wickedly infectious.

They hang on to their night-time right up to the summer solstice, and they carry it through to the summer holidays.

With them, the night-time kids, we can glimpse from November on, and from a fair distance, the solitary blinking of the wind turbines.

In the morning, we can tell how much time we've got before high school starts from the barn lights, because only the barns are lit up, along with a few sections of road, illuminated by the headlights.

Some evenings, we have to stop and get out of the bus to return dazed calves to the fields, after they've got under the electric fence without realising, and can no longer work out what's what, because of the noise, the scent of their mother, and the headlights of the bus. They are distraught and already so heavy and muscular that we need two or three of us to push them. We laugh about the athletic stupidity of the calves, about the darkness, grumbling for the sake of it.

On the outskirts of the forest, we watch as baby goats take fright, their velvety bums reflecting the moon or the low-beam headlights like the flickering light from a mirror.

Sometimes we see apparitions of unrecognisable animals, or of supernormal meteorological phenomena. I love my teenagers for this too, I like that about them, those nights together.

~

Lise is like them, it's strange, she has already entered the night, perhaps that's why she hasn't said hello, or else it's because of her arm gesture. I can imagine how embarrassed she is about her new asymmetrical breasts. I'm getting everything mixed up in my zigzag bends and thoughts. Her gesture is one that marks the beginning of adolescence, but also the end, because it's the gesture of a woman. There's a kind of premonition in the movement of the arm.

One evening, my two Loire kids and I saw a lunar rainbow together. I was running a bit late and, at the foot of the mountain, I really wanted to slow down, the moon was so huge and full in the still-damp night after all the rain during the day. Just before the second-last stop, just before dropping off Nielle, after a slight rise, we passed beneath a lunar rainbow of infinite splendour, its bows arching up from the plateau. I had never seen one before. Majestic, grey, strange, no sappy colours, half on its side like a solar rainbow, but with those beautiful vertical colours: greys, blacks, whites. A lunar rainbow, rising above us, and we passed beneath it.

(on the way back from the high school)

The last of the logging trucks are heading from the other direction, pulling out wide into the oncoming lane on the corners, which forces me to slow down. They let out their bullish blasts of air along these uncomfortable, scarred roads. I let one, two go past, then I move the bus back into the middle of the road.

The setting sun on the dirty windows bothers me and makes me feel unnaturally tired. I always feel weaker in the sun than on overcast days, or in the night. When it's dark at dawn, I'm at my best.

My big kids are quiet. I think they're exhausted too. It's often like this on the first day—after the excitement of the morning, it's as if they're sick of it all, disappointed.

Seeing them sad every year on the evening of the first day back at school makes me feel uneasy, disconnected from myself. I can't escape the feeling that I have led them away from their own expectations.

When I was a little boy, I wanted to go to Sunday school, and it wasn't even just to be like the others. I wanted answers to my questions, I was a bit mystical, ill at ease in my body, and above all I loved the rituals of the mass. I couldn't stop thinking about communion, I wanted to receive the body of Christ, to swallow it, drink his blood. My brother made fun of me, but he was prepared to go into the village with me.

Maman tried to respond to my obsessive questions, to which I had still not received answers after Sunday school and the priest's explanations. Why is it us inside our bodies? What is the after that comes after death? Where does the infinite world finish? And, for that matter, where does it begin? And how do you eat the word of God? Maman had her own ideas on the question of miracles, for example. According to her, the loaves were not multiplied by Jesus, but distributed under his influence. All he had to do was to convince people to share. If someone gets out the crust of bread they've hidden away and offers it to others, everyone will do the same thing, everyone has a little bit of something to share. See, it's simple, it's human nature. God is human. And you know the word *companion*, well, that's what it means, the person you eat bread with.

Except that the priest got angry with me when I came back to class with these interpretations. He wasn't as intelligent as my mother, so it wasn't worth going anymore. My brother, who used to escort me to the door of the presbytery, told me to drop the whole thing. Come and see, he said. He took me by the hand, walked me to a nearby porch and pushed me inside. Don't be frightened, he said. Through the archway, we entered a vaulted cellar and in the centre, on the beaten-earth floor, was an enormous ossuary. A pile of bones bigger and taller than we were. For weeks we kept going there, in secret. (We said we were going to Bible study, which was almost true.) We revelled in the mysteries of the ossuary, intoxicated by our extravagant speculations, by doing what we were sure was

forbidden—crossing the threshold of the cellar—
and by the lie we shared.

I'm through the pass and Nielle sees him first. Nielle
who is always away with the fairies, his head in the
clouds, on Mars, anywhere else but in the here and
now. Adèle, that guy over there, is that him?

There, right after the pass, just where the
highway narrows dangerously between two vertical
rock faces, leaning against a buttress-shaped
boulder the size of a human body, but very close to
the narrow road, was our old crazy guy from five
years ago, our reckless idiot with the balaclava.

Wednesday,
26th October

(on the way to the high school)

The autumn you read about in books doesn't last. The flamboyant colours, the lyrical oranges of the beech trees, the brilliant ochres of the willows, the sun-speckled acid greens on the birches, the deep reds bleeding into scarlet of the maple forests, or conversely the sparkling, pointillist reds of the individual maples standing out among the yellows of the other trees—there's just time for me to describe it, time for the wind to send a few leaves back to the ground, and two or three more trips with my kids, and it's over. It's over on the ground as well as on the branches.

By the side of the road the colour scheme of the leaves is reduced to a narrow range of browns, and the trunks are already greyish pink. Not a romance-novel pink, no, a dull pink, and then higher up in the twigs and branches are the dirty purples. The higher up we go, more of those recessive violet shades appear, dirty, violet hues, along with sickly pinks that are simultaneously pale and dark, but so muted that our pupils dilate in order to see them there.

On my trips, autumn is soon enough a display of dreary colours that match the fog. Fog everywhere, from the soil right up to the trees, infiltrating the bark. When the fog is a blanket all around us, our pupils become enormous. I have the reassuring impression that everything is in place, that the forest is finally as it should be, once the sun and those pitiful pinks have been dispelled.

After driving through the forests of fog, we reach a high, flat plain with scraggy shrubs. At the end of the day, a perfectly horizontal band of light shoots out at ground level and extends to the edge of the plateau, but the rest of the time the sun is grey. The peaks intersect with the plains, which are drab, slate-coloured and almost dusty, almost silvery, but in the end never anything other than a sad greyness. Except, except for a strange phenomenon, a swift silvery flash, when the undersides of the leaves, before they darken, appear shiny and remain in the mind as a jewel-like exception to the misfortunes of the plateau.

We dive down along the bare plateau, climb up again, and then head into the far-off distance. So far that the people in the fields look like flickering emotions of the earth, so far that it's beautiful, but not because of nature. Nature is like all the rest, it's no more beautiful or more pure than a city, than shopping centres or industrial areas, than the haughty wind turbines soaring over the spruce trees. Sometimes even nature is just that: irritating and overwrought, so ugly and dirty in autumn, muddy and slimy in spring when the snow gets sticky, arrogant with winter's flawless sun, and ridiculously green in summer. Difficult, annoying, like all the rest.

If, nevertheless, I often find the plateau around me so beautiful, it's only because I live here. It's stupid, but the place where one lives is magnificent. It depends how you get up in the morning, the way you look outside; it depends on whether you do look outside. There are some days, mornings or evenings, when the weather in the landscape, the atmosphere in the trees, is exactly, in an almost crass way, in harmony with the weather in our bodies, with the atmosphere in our moods: we're gloomy and it is outside too, moisture is palpable everywhere, from our bodies to far in the distance as well, further than we can see, since the drizzle obscures our vision. It even takes us by surprise in the kitchen, and we were especially looking forward to being there. That the rain is cold on our necks does not take away our desire to cry, but it makes our depression almost sweeter.

Yesterday, oddly enough, it was a huge transparent sun that appeared through my tears, and it worked the same way: my tears were clear, luminous. To duplicate our own moods with the climate of things is a relief for us everywhere, as long as everywhere is here where we live.

To my right, on the front seat, Sébastien is bending over to rummage in his schoolbag. Nadège is lost in concentration, her head leaning against the fogged-up window. She is sitting up front, next to him, but she is in another world, far away from us. This morning the weather is abnormally mild, with warm mist carried by an almost unbearably fierce and acrid-smelling south wind. Two days ago, though, it was minus twelve at the beginning of the trip, too cold for snow. The old people have already begun cutting broom shrubs in order to insulate the roofs of the chicken coops. When I picked up the little kids, Hugues carried into the bus with him the smell of hay and cold cream, as he told me proudly: I helped Maman feed the heifers.

We are used to that temperature gap, and to the wind, but still it worries me.

I don't think the condensation on the window today is either cold or hot on Nadège's cheek. I also know that at her age things often work in reverse: nowhere is the place where you live. Nowhere, because of that difficulty in adolescence of being so suddenly and so violently sexualised. But perhaps it's easier for her. Yes, I think it must be easier, when your gender is more or less unequivocal. She sits up suddenly, comes back to earth, and smiles at me over the top of Sébastien, because his whole head is now in his bag (I forgot my history homework: the teacher's going to kill me).

I'm not absolutely sure it's easier. I remember just a bit too much about my own adolescence, about the misery I had to endure, how it seemed insurmountable. I would like to tell this to Nadège. But how can I talk to her? It's impossible to talk, even to Nadège, who either spreads her legs or keeps them squeezed tight. I would like to say to her: No one's stopping you from spreading your legs, but no one's making you do it. I can't explain to her how I could neither spread my legs nor keep them together. In order to become who I was, a girl, I locked myself in the bathroom. I had only limited time to myself. During the rest of the time, and space, I had to carry my genitals in front of me in order to look as if I was what I wasn't, a boy, and there was the added irritation of being attractive to girls because of my idiotic romantic appearance, the same air that Sébastien is trying to adopt now as, resigned, he closes his schoolbag and looks at Nadège, then turns to me, then back to her.

See, Adèle, Nadège couldn't care less about my suffering, she's thinking about something or other, but I'm going to be killed by my teacher, she couldn't care less, look at her. Whispering, he turns to her. And yet the other night, while the stags were rutting, she wasn't playing hard to get…you haven't forgotten already, have you, my doe-eyed darling?

I keep looking straight ahead at the road, but I smile at him, and I understand that in his mind Nadège is a little bit like me.

Nadège sighs as she wipes Sébastien's nose. She rubs the specks of dirt off him, and tells him to blow his nose in clean leaves next time. Sébastien addresses me as he turns round to Joël to make fun of him:

You know, it's *ecological*, Adèle? They're autumn handkerchiefs, they come in all different colours, you'll like the softness of the new oak-leaf handkerchief, and the velvety quality of our new collection, Feels Like Cashmere, autumn handkerchiefs, disposable handkerchiefs, disposable anywhere. The Maries laugh, everyone laughs, and I realise that the wind has dropped.

The wind is the worst thing about here. The wind is almost always here, gusting, and never from the same direction. The wind turns, loses its bearings, and doesn't settle. Wind without snow is not quite wind, yet it's not a blizzard, it doesn't count for as much, but it is part of our domain, part of us. When the blizzard arrives, it will be almost the opposite, we will be part of the wind, snowed in and stormed.

The rest of the world is there, in motion, with a noise that silences all other noise. Ocean fronts, abysses, cities, unimaginable borders are here, in the wind. Waves of wind furrow the fields, smooth out the colours of the heather and blow away all the acidity of the ferns. The wind lays down ridges on the new beech branches, on the flat expanse of the lakes, on the grey bark of the thirty-year-old ash trees. There are creases everywhere, even on people's cheeks.

Nielle, who hardly ever speaks, comments on this particular silence, or rather on the absence of noise. I see him in the rear-vision mirror, sitting up to look out the window. Sylvain removes his hood and Sébastien whispers: It's stopped. Everyone knows that the two or three seconds of nothing that follow the halting of things, of wind, of time, are an expansion, no, a retraction of the world before catastrophes—so-called natural—cliffs that collapse onto ocean beaches, earthquakes, oceanic rifts, floods, volcanic eruptions.

A painful cramping of landmasses.

I remember my birth. I'm not the only one, almost everyone remembers their birth, but almost no one cares much about it, that's all. I know about it because, when I recover the sensations that accompanied my birth, I find it unbearable. There's not much to go on, only a few things: the memory of the birth canal. My whole body crushed, vibrating with the contractions, quite literally a panic attack, reverberating all over, returning now, still—when I'm in the gorges, in the fog, but also in full sunlight, in a gust of wind, in the middle of intercourse, when a man doesn't hold himself up properly on his elbows and crushes my breasts.

In one of his letters, my brother was telling me about custom-made components designed according to the shape of the rock, formwork moulds, reinforced-concrete supports to retain the slabs of rocks. I made a drawing of the mountain's corset.

~

Oddly enough, being squeezed, held, makes me feel good, as long as it's not by a person. I don't like loose-fitting clothes. Almost every night, I crouch in a narrow bathtub (when I moved to the village, I was so happy to find a bathtub like that in the apartment—my size, I told myself). I sleep wedged between the bed and the wall, my right arm and leg under the mattress. When I was a little boy, I used to ride my bike for kilometres through the plateau overflowing with fireweed. My tyres caught in the bulky purple stalks; in some spots they were taller than I was, but I didn't want to go all the way around on the road. I would extricate myself, and climb back on my bike. Sometimes I would carry it so I could reach the open fields, where I pedalled as hard as I could in order to shake off my brother and feel the huge, thick stubble left from the haymaking scrape against my tyres. I used to hurtle along towards the volcano to swim in the icy lake, my lake, my break, to have the sensation of my body cramping, to let my skin, gripped by the cold, be lashed by the water. I would swim towards the centre, let myself sink a bit (and my brother would yell out, terrified, standing up on the pedals of his bike—we'd be killed if Maman found out). But I was the one who was terrified if he got me in a headlock when we were playing. He used to have fun wrestling me to the ground, and winding me with nothing more than his body weight. I would run, suffocating, to get Maman. Baffled, my brother would declare that we were just play-fighting.

When what is holding me, confining me, is someone else's body—instead of my own, or water, or things—that's when I get frightened, I feel sick, I get cold, stressed.

As a woman now, I hate being held by someone else. As a boy, I always found it painful to be sodomised, and I already thought it was because of my harrowing birth. And yet I enjoyed, I enjoy, vaginal penetration, even with the new scar tissue on my labia. I enjoyed it straight away, a few weeks after the operation. (I didn't follow the medical advice to wait four months, I'd felt ready for such a long time.) I enjoy it, and feel no pain, until a man orgasms and collapses on me. Then it's not the same thing at all. Get off, I'm suffocating.

~

I often let myself be sodomised, because I like men, but it always left me feeling cold. As a boy I felt cold, as a girl I felt cold. As a girl, I was in some pain, torn of course, but most of all I felt cold, my whole being retracted, frozen several times over, as if through several layers, as if deep inside myself, like, ah yes, like the mountain stream beneath the caves two years ago: the water froze gradually, deeper and deeper, slowed and stopped flowing, until the currents in the depths froze. In the end there were series of haphazard layers of motionless waves.

When, as a boy, I was sodomised, I felt, as a girl, both assaulted and misshapen, I felt dual, and it made me want to vomit. I have no idea why. I couldn't manage being conscious of myself as a girl, a girl being penetrated from behind.

One day, I thrashed about as if the guy was raping me. He stopped immediately, amazed, but gentle. He tried to reassure me, but I had no idea what I was frightened of, what was causing me so much pain, what was making me feel so cold. As a boy I felt inexplicably knocked about; as a girl I felt brutalised. As a boy I felt forsaken and as a girl I felt subjected to an indecent intimacy. I was also bothered by something strange: I was distressed about staying pressed against this guy like a brother, a Siamese sister. It was ridiculous, excessive, and this time really horrendous, and yet my penis became erect, I got hard, disgusted as a girl by my boy's body.

As a boy, I put my clothes back on, and, as a girl, I sat down, to tell this guy a story I'd heard on the radio. It was the story of two Siamese sisters, one body and two heads. One of them got married and the other one pressed charges against her for rape, indecent assault, false imprisonment, aggravated procurement. The guy lost his temper. What a load of rubbish, that's got nothing to do with anything. He called me crazy, sick, sexually disabled.

No one is speaking. Through the window, the earth looks like a closed fist.

Perhaps I'm over-interpreting the silence as I drive, the bus rolling along on a surface that doesn't seem quite normal to me, but I'd like to pull over for safety's sake. I decide to park the bus. But perhaps the catastrophe will happen while I'm trying to find a spot. I know it, and my big kids, who remain stubbornly silent, know it too.

I turn off the motor, as if the silence were not already too vast and oppressive.

The gorges are not far away, but the noise took a while to get here. Perhaps five or six seconds.

Joël is the first to react, one sentence:

Shit, the one time I remembered to bring my art materials.

Tuesday,
15th November

(on the way to the high school)

The wind only started back up this morning, nineteen days after the landslide. Almost three weeks without wind, it's so rare. More than ever, gossip gathered about the weather. There were several hypotheses: volcanic mountains of words not said, breath stifled, the windless mountain's silent remorse; some suggested climate change was the cause; the old people shrugged and the same tired line came out of their mouths, so hackneyed that its currency is universal. They shrugged: There are no seasons anymore.

Just before it was time to leave, the wind dumped piles of swirling snow, and with the snowstorm came the same old fears of the people here, the same century-old expressions, and straight after that the snowdrifts start to form, in the same places as last year, and I wonder why I haven't been told to take an alternative route.

I get a bit irritable on the mountain, the bus gets bogged, but my Loire kids remain calm, and their calmness settles me. Nielle warns me about the snow plough just behind us. I let it pass and then steer the bus into its tracks.

On the Friday of the accident, the noise of the choppers echoed around the mountain until late into the evening. All that racket for a single casualty.

This Sunday, when I entered the warmth and calm of the hospital room, I couldn't help making fun (my turn now) of my brother, of how ludicrously exhausted he looked, of that oversized splint on his index finger.

He defended himself by explaining slowly, very slowly, in order to demonstrate to me properly what a stupid woman I was, that several more operations were still needed on his fingers.

And I've already been operated on twice, he said. Just because the finger took the brunt of the injury doesn't mean that it's not serious. Without my hand I can't work, it means at least six months off work. I'm going to have to go to the physio every day for I don't know how long. If you haven't figured that out, you're a really dumb bitch. And if I try to wiggle my thumbs and index finger, ah, very funny, whatever, there's no way I'm going to put up with being paid to do nothing, not me, I'm not just some chick driving the school bus.

He paused. How come you're only visiting me now?

He was asking me the question out of left field, because I only came to see him three weeks after his accident, and we haven't seen each other for over a decade.

I love it when my little brother is in a bad mood. And my smile told him that I had noticed—noticed that during his argument with me, for the first time, without being pressured to, naturally (he who used to say to me, what you're going to do is not natural, it's sick), he had made the correct gender agreement, several times.

He had already done it before, of course, but only under social pressure, when he couldn't speak to me as a male without provoking a lot of questions.

One day he will call me by my new name; one day I'll be his big sister Adèle.

We were living together when they flooded the bottom farm. We were teenagers, and already old orphans. Maman had been dead a long time, and Papa continued to live (and would eventually die) in a sort of asylum, rest home, where time dragged on forever, and even more so during the Sunday-night card games of coinche.

After burying my mother, after selling up all the cows, my father rented out the land, then caved in very quickly to the electricity company's haggling. He accepted their deal without fuss, and then fell into a ferocious depression. His voice was ravaged by years of tobacco and silence. He could scarcely utter a word anymore. So the three of us were living off that money without doing anything with the bottom farm. There were still a few chooks as well as the pig, just for Papa to have something to do. We also took five or six draught horses on agistment when the snows melted.

My brother and I were only there on weekends, then only one weekend in two—we were boarders from high school on, as if we were on agistment too.

For a long time I had been thinking of myself in the feminine, making all the grammatical gender agreements in my mind. But as I was well and truly the only female in this situation, I felt both lonely and not in agreement with myself.

We arrived home late on Friday nights (two, then later three, bus changes). Papa hugged us, clasping bits of paper, which he slipped hesitantly into our open hands. It reminded me of when Grandma would slip money to us in secret, trembling. First she reprimanded us: Well? Take it, I'm giving it to you! And don't go telling the others, and make sure you don't spend it on rubbish. Papa would scrunch up the bits of paper as he stuffed them into the palms of our hands; warm, damp scraps like worn-out promises.

They were lists of things to do. Maman used to write them for us every Sunday for the week to come, lists of chores that weren't really chores. But there was almost nothing on Papa's lists, which meant we invented tasks for ourselves so that he wouldn't notice, so that he would never find us lost in thought, idle.

If he approached me, his eyes brimming with tears, I would get up, answer his wordless pleas. I'm coming, I'm coming. And when I didn't know where, where to go, I always went to see the horses, our agisted horses.

I really loved going to see the horses, hearing them well before I saw them. Not just hearing them, but all the senses in my body tuned to the sound and weight of them, through the ground, for hundreds of metres all around. I liked walking on the ample, elongated vibrations they made. I let myself shudder in their hoofmarks, brushing aside the clumps of soil that were heavy, too, and rough.

I was reading a book that I couldn't get out of my head. I had borrowed it from school because it was about battling a mountain flood. I was obsessed with the book and had decided never to return it. There was a wonderful passage in which an old woman was gored, shaken, disembowelled, ripped to shreds, trampled on by a huge bull clambering out of the waters that had inundated the fields. I don't know why or how, but the violence of that death was a comfort to me, a part of me felt better. At the sound of the horses, that passage resurfaced in my body, and one night, in earshot of the horses, I vowed to myself that I would choose the name of that old woman when I was reborn, hoping to end up all wizened like her, tiny, in a wild hand-to-hand embrace with the shifting landscape.

I would daydream, make up amazing films in my head, all the while pretending to help Papa.

I was in Year Twelve when we had to come to terms with the fact that my father was no longer even washing himself. By the time social services got involved, and we pretended to resist for a bit, it was all arranged. The family said they wanted to take him, but we weren't sure exactly who; no one really volunteered, and the waters were already rising slowly around the farm. The asylum was really the most practical solution, avoiding any domestic issues. It was down below us, in the city, so my brother and I just had to move nearby, there you go, it's all sorted, hey, boys, it's for the best. Near Papa, near school, near uni.

Yes, it was convenient, except that I had never been a boy, and this city, so far away from our farm, from the hamlet, from the village, meant only one thing for me: I could become who I was, without anyone noticing, or telling tales on me, or making a big deal about it.

I was thrilled. It felt indecent because of Papa, but I was a happy girl.

With the money from the hydroelectricity company, we moved into a place in the centre of the city. We set ourselves up like a student couple. It was a minuscule furnished apartment, cluttered with countless bits and pieces, knick-knacks, and the owner's doll collection. It was kitsch and bordering on squalid, with only one bedroom. We took it in turns to sleep on the couch, week about, and we shared the chores, just like on the farm. I swept, washed the dishes, did the cooking, the laundry. Honestly, I quite like doing the laundry, you do it alone, even the sorting. (I don't know where I read it, but it was a character in a novel who called these chores the handiwork of angels, domestic gestures that get performed automatically.)

After school Axel tinkered at home, he fixed leaks, anything that was falling apart, and there was a lot of it. One day he drilled a groove along the walls so he could rewire the electrics. I told him he was crazy, there was dust everywhere, he was covered in it, all grey and white. He wiped his hand over his eyelids, and the look that emerged from this gesture was mysterious and alive.

I loved our life together. I started to change my body like a blouse, every morning and every night. I spent hours on it. When we were due to visit our father, my brother reminded me days beforehand, as if I might not have time to take off my make-up and remove my splints and trellises. He always used odd words like that.

It's true I took my time, but it was time out, time for me, time for me to get my bearings, to fashion myself the way I wanted to be, malleable time that gave me confidence as a girl. I tucked my penis beneath the hitched-up skin of my testicles, or in the cleft of my buttocks, determined to keep it absolutely in the middle of my body, rather than to the left or right. I was shaping myself into a girl, I had been doing it for a long time, but it was no longer in secret, quick and dirty, I was no longer terrified of being caught. So I took my time, I drew my penis back slowly and carefully. I stretched my skin the way you would cover a sleeping body with a blanket, out of modesty, not out of fear that it might catch cold.

My brother would get annoyed waiting on the other side of the bathroom door. We argued because he thought I was an indecent boy, when I was trying to be a suitably attired girl, in a corset and tight girdle. (I bought them in sex shops or in second-hand shops.) For him, I was too much of an indecent, old-fashioned boy to be a girl. He'd whisper: A bra is enough, even though you've got nothing to put inside it, your pads are empty, they're just foam. He didn't dare say it loudly—for once we had neigh-bours. Actually, for the neighbours we had to act as if I was a girl, and as I could not be my brother's big sister (he had never had a sister and never would have one), without discussing it we had assumed the roles people expected of us, that of a young couple who happened to look like each other.

The visits to my father became less frequent, then his depression worsened, ravaged him, to the point that he no longer recognised us.

For three years, in front of other people, my brother made an effort to speak to me as if I was female, to be affectionate, attentive, and then, behind closed doors, when I was male in his eyes, he was insensitive, aggressive, sometimes violent.

I knew what to expect when I got home, but I didn't care, I felt so good as a girl, almost happy. The hormone treatments were tiring but beneficial, they were bringing my body back to life for me— via a gradual wasting of my muscles that I used to measure eagerly in the big mirror in the hallway. The treatments restored that body to me, the body

I had missed in every sense—I felt stabs of joy between my legs, in my emerging shoulder blades (I used to twist around to see them finally appearing), between my budding breasts. My brother would push and shove the woman's body swivelling in the hallway. I had missed that body for so long that sometimes, even now, I still feel reverberations of missing it, a throbbing.

When I was a little boy, I often dreamed that I had a slit, and then I would wake up disappointed. I was too young to understand, I thought it was like what Maman used to say when I was clumsy: You don't have any legs. In my little boy's mind, I imagined myself as a mermaid, the little mermaid whose story I begged for every night, who, for the sake of love, allowed her tail to be split and become human legs. I had my mother read it and explain it over and over, until sometimes she lost patience. I'd ask: So do you have to be a woman to be in love? Do you have to have a slit?

Oh, you're so stupid, my mother would reply. You can still love with a willy. You're a little boy, she's a female fish, do you understand?

But later, when I'm a bigger boy, I'll be split into a girl too, won't I?

No, not at all, my darling, don't be afraid.

I didn't want to disappoint her, so I made myself visualise my penis before going to sleep, so I would dream correctly. One night, I managed to have a girl's dream in which I was a girl, but a girl with a penis, a girl's penis, not a clitoris, a long, slender, translucent phallus, a young girl's penis. I knew much later that it was a girl's dream when girlfriends—girls by birth—told me about similar dreams.

In the apartment in the city, I was taking shape, I had lovers, and most importantly, most importantly for others, I was my brother's wife. And I loved him intensely, even though the whole business was madness. He was frightened. With all the pointless and puerile arguments he could muster, he resisted his mates' invitations. Come on, you and your girl-friend, come and have a drink. What revision, the exams are over, don't be an idiot. The worst or the best was when his mates invited themselves over to our place, and we had to pretend to sleep together.

I loved him so intensely, I was so happy and he was so miserable that one night I begged him just to tell everyone what the situation was. Through his tears he told me he would rather people thought we were a couple—that they didn't know the rest of it. He said that, *the rest of it*, because he was never able to talk about my transvestism, or my trans-sexuality, or my real identity, because that *rest of it* was unthinkable, he'd rather die, rather die than talk about it. His crying was so unrestrained it made me feel nauseous. He was furious about being made vulnerable.

One evening I took him in my arms, and noticed that he stopped talking. He buried himself in my foam puffs, as he called them, and then he resumed his furious sobbing:

You'll never be my sister, no, that will never happen, but you know I love you—you know that when I don't speak to you, when I don't say anything at all, that's what I mean. When I press against you now and there's something missing, I understand that it's you I miss. I miss you, you have no idea. I miss my big brother. You'll never be my sister, but I will always be your little brother, so I don't mind kissing you on the neck in front of other people, because that's what I did with Maman, so it's no big deal, it doesn't mean anything else.

We separated because Axel went back to his passion for rock climbing. He changed cities, he enrolled in adult-education classes to obtain his certification and to take the medical fitness test for rope access work. I stayed for a short while in the apartment that had been rewired by my brother. I dropped out of uni, I did odd jobs in order to save enough money for the operation. I had all the tests, I went to the shrinks, and I took the train alone to Brussels.

When I had my new identity card in my hands, I stared for ages at the little *f* and at my new first name. I could have wept with happiness. I wanted to go back and wander around the bottom farm for a day or two, my legs walking on my own soil, go back with my slit to the lake where I had been my mother's little mermaid.

I did go back to the plateau. I drove up and walked down until I reached the bottom farm. They had drained the lake in order to get rid of the stones. It was unimaginable, dangerous, terrifying. I took my time walking down, I had brand-new walking shoes that must have made me look like a tourist. The weather was unusual: no sun, no rain, no wind, no fog, no snow, but all of them lurking in the motionless clouds. The sun shone through fissures in the clouds—it must have been sunlight—and more than fissures, the clouds were opening up, opening up along a seam that was simultaneously wispy and distended, as if the skin on the clouds that day was taut, had been grazed repeatedly, and was bleeding a sort of luminous, sweaty, almost viscous lymphatic fluid that hurt your eyes when you looked at it.

There were a few walkers, hikers and fishermen along the sandy banks of the newly emerged river. Dusty sand, not even silt, instead of our peat bog, instead of our mud brimming with smells. I sat down on what was left of the trees on the shore and I breathed in memories. But they didn't really come back to me. What did resurface was a single image, like a photograph, of our gumboots left in a jumble in the entrance hall of the house. Perhaps also some physical sensations, fleeting sensations of our indefatigable and foolhardy footsteps in the peat, in the snow, in the waterlogged fields. In pockets of stagnant river water there was sometimes a layer of ice crammed with leaves and shadows. I used to walk in, so that I could hear the screech, the melting, and so that the feeling of the mud squelching beneath my boots would reach up my calves.

My brother preferred climbing up above the tide pool and hurling himself into the skating rinks of ice that formed in autumn before the snow, when it was too cold for snowfalls. The contours of the fields retained the late-September rain, frozen by the icy weather and sprinkled with sleet. We used to run around, ignoring the cows, and the time, only coming to a skidding halt at the metal hay racks, panting like wild animals, then the two of us started up our stampede again, Maman's fears gone from our minds.

~

I stood up when I saw one of our old neighbours. He greeted me. (I felt as fractured as the clouds.) He came over. Like all old people laden with memories, he started talking, and talking…He had a bellyful of memories, sorrows and joys heaped together, so crowded that they overflowed into my own past. First he pointed out the clouds, interrogating me about the weather forecast, then he told me the story of my family, going back to a time I thought I had forgotten. He mimed, with emphatic, exaggerated gestures, the way my father used to roll the logs from the upper valley down to the farm.

We used to call it the bottom farm well before the waters rose, you know, because, look, the farm is right in the middle of the crater.

I could tell that he hadn't recognised me. I savoured that accent, his accent, my accent chewed over by this old man, I wanted to open my mouth wide—to drink it in, gulp it down, take it back.

You see, the tractor couldn't drag the tree trunks all the way down to the bottom, it was too difficult, it got bogged in the mud, wretched thing, so he unloaded them on the side of the path up there (he pointed to the path, where I was already looking). He gave them a shove, and they rolled with one hell of a roar, you can imagine it.

I didn't imagine it, no, I remembered it. I remembered the mighty low-pitched rolling of the naked trunks, then the chainsaw's shrill echo, and the enormous piles of stacked wood under tarpaulins along the walls. But I had no memory of ever having an axe or a wood splitter in my hand; doing the wood was on my brother's list. Cutting, splitting, carrying, stacking.

My father would sometimes even take him along to the wood harvesting, to cut down the trees and chop up the trunks. But not me, I was too clumsy, and Maman needed me in the house.

Ah, yes, just like that (he kept on with his dramatic gestures).

And then afterwards the logs had to be chopped again, split, carried and stacked in front of the house. A wood fire is a warm fire. There were three wooden stoves to fill, then the kitchen fireplace, the kitchen range. (The logs had to be re-split into kindling, I was allowed to do that.)

In front of the blue-grey barn door, the sawdust mixed with mud froze at the first frosts, and our dirt courtyard ended up with a brittle and gritty surface like papier-mâché, which I used to try to flatten out with my boots when I got bored sulking outside. In a calm fury, I trampled our ice-encrusted ground, and it sent me into a soothing contemplation, of what I have no idea now.

You don't understand, you young people, you use oil for heating, but soon there won't be any more oil, I'm telling you, he said (with the accent).

He regained his composure and pointed to the blue-grey door of the barn, the door my father had made out of bits of an aeroplane. He asked me if I knew what it was made out of. I lied and said no, just so I could hear him tell the story we were so proud of.

During the last war a plane crashed right next to the farm, it wasn't yesterday, eh, it was when his grandparents were alive. The grandparents spent weeks chopping up the plane, and no one touched the pieces for years.

He told me how my father, almost inadvertently, had patched up an old door with bits of the aeroplane. He looked pleased with himself, as if he admired my father, even if it was reluctantly. He went quiet for a few moments before telling me that there were plenty more stories about this house, plenty more, oh yes, my dear, you have no idea.

He wanted to tell me more: you deserve a drink for listening so well, yes, come on, I'd like that. On the way back to the hamlet by car with him, I looked people in the eye, and no one, no one at all, recognised me. I went into the bar. I came face to face with almost everything and everyone I'd known, and that world of my past looked at me as if I was a stranger, and as if I was a woman, but with a sort of benevolence that I never knew existed there.

I went back to get my car and drove to the village.

No one in the village recognised me either. I checked into a hotel and played the role of the new woman in town. I played the role of the woman who liked the mountains and was looking for a job, and I still had a bit of the local accent, and a name that reminded them of another name. (Are you related to the people from the bottom farm? No?) The municipal association gave me a job, and even found me somewhere to live, almost immediately, near the local park. A month later, as planned, I returned with my suitcases. I moved into an apartment above the swings.

Every morning when I went to buy my eggs and yoghurt, the woman at the grocer's was anxious. The snow? The snow's nothing, it's the wind, my dear, that's the problem. Every morning she began by calling me a brave woman, and she even, often, called me an early bird (and when she said it, it was with admiration).

I've been driving the bus ever since. Among themselves, hardly ever in front of me, the kids call me driver, but it's not even pejorative. I am the local driver, their big brothers' driver. It's already been about ten years. I'm alone up here. When I have problems, or affairs, flings, lovers, it's always down in town. Up here I'm alone, but content.

Once again, the landscape has filled up my whole being. My countryside is contained within me, it fulfils me, it is enough.

For ten years I've been living a lie, a secret kept by the mountains, but not really. It's been a long time since those first sideways glances and the latest tittle-tattle. I feel accepted, I go by the first name I chose all that time ago, from the book about the old woman in the flood. I am the woman I have always been, except that I can't say it.

At the hospital the day before yesterday, I was wondering about all that, and I thought everyone would start to speculate now, ten years later, that they would ask questions, about my relationship with Axel, about the orphan child of the plateau who came back and got injured in the reinforcement works (it's written here, in last week's newspaper).

I put away the newspaper. My brother seemed really tired.

Everyone is going to know immediately that I came to see him in the hospital and, because our surnames are the same, I know people will put two and two together in no time at all and the news will spread everywhere.

Yesterday the kids didn't mention anything about it to me, but it won't be long, I'm sure. I look at

Nielle and Sylvain, half asleep, silent. I can't see the snow plough anymore, but I'm in its tracks, I'm feeling confident.

On Sunday, my brother was falling asleep. I kept vigil like a real big sister. He nodded off the way you sleep in hospital, in time with the odd rhythm of a clock that's out of sync. I love hospitals, I find them comforting, I've always felt calm there, even when Maman died. It was here, as a matter of fact—and I was ashamed by how reassured I felt. I've never been conventional. That's what my father used to say, when he came across me putting on Maman's clothes, or even Grandma's clothes, he said that I deserved a beating, but Maman said, Let it go, he'll get over it before it's a problem, and he never hit me.

My brother opened his eyes, I asked him how he felt, he smiled and blushed as he told me that he felt at ease without knowing why, and when I smiled too, he reminded me of what I already knew, that Maman was dead and she died in this hospital.

We should go and see Papa a bit more often, don't

you think, Adèle? How long since you've been?

I paused. Every now and then, when I felt disoriented, I couldn't be sure anymore whether my father was still alive. Axel stared at me, a look verging on terror. Perhaps I was going to take it the wrong way, whatever he was about to say. But considering how long it had been on his mind, that baby…

It was not an embryo like all those others, he said, all the ones she lost, don't you remember how big it was?

No, I don't want to talk about that at all.

Oh, yeah, that's taboo for you, you're such a liberated *woman*.

Stop it, Axel.

No, I'm not going to stop, I won't stop, and for once it's you who's going to look at things squarely, see them for what they are.

He went quiet all of a sudden, because I'd shivered when he said *things* instead of *bodies* (embryos, foetuses)—of our little brothers and sisters, of our little brothers or sisters, of Maman's body, her womb that was so fluky (flexible, floppy). We never knew exactly how many pregnancies she'd had, there were some before us and some after us, there were so many of them, and only two children who lived, only us.

My brother started talking again, quietly, his tone almost affectionate:

You know, for a long time I thought that was why you…well, you know what I mean, but then I realised that wasn't it, that had nothing to do with what you did. I'm not that stupid, you know, I'm not like those morons with their simplistic pop psychology, now I know perfectly well that it has nothing to do with it.

He stared at me; there was both complicity and mistrust in his gaze.

But you can't say all that didn't form us, deform us, I don't know, it made us who we are, in any case, that's what we're made of, you and me, and I want to know, yes, I want to know if that one, the last one, was a girl or a boy, because that's the one that killed Maman, and him too, or her, who knows, it died too, when I'm certain the foetus was viable. Why don't we know whether it was a brother or a sister? Why didn't we bury it? Why didn't we ever say that it wasn't his or her fault? That it was nobody's fault, that it was because of that wretched bottom farm, because of the snow, the snowstorm. Don't you remember the storm that day, in that hillbilly hole, that shithole of a plateau held together by nothing more than anti-submarine nets. For fuck's sake, we lived too far from everything, we should have called a chopper, there were three of them around for me on Friday, for a finger, didn't you hear the damn noise they were making in the gorges and all over the plateau, you must have heard it, were you deaf?

I tried to reply through tears and snot, but it was too painful because of all the memories resurfacing, pale and mucousy, still sticky with all that stuff, memories of spring snow, dull grey, slippery, dangerous mud everywhere; in our neck of the woods, when we say spring snow, we know exactly what that means, because spring is just a less harsh winter and therefore more snow, more wind and only slightly less cold.

It was spring when Maman died, my brother continued, it was spring when Maman went into labour, she didn't die in hospital, she didn't even die on the way there, we brought her here, to the hospital, two days later, I have no idea why, probably for an autopsy.

When she started to bleed, I said, it was during a snowstorm, you said so yourself, you remember it, and yet how old were you? There's no spring snow plough that can clear the road fast enough, the snow's too sticky, snow cutters are even slower, and how do you expect choppers to fly and then land in a snowstorm like that? Down on the bottom farm the snow always swirled like crazy, you know how we even called it the cyclone, where the lake is now, we used to say, I live on the bottom farm, in the cyclone.

My brother smiled as he recalled how proud we were, as little boys, to live in the cyclone. He hasn't cried since his accident. He was about to the day before yesterday, but his tears subsided, and anyway mine were enough. I certainly cried enough for two, even three, so then we started laughing, laughing like lunatics, and I said to myself that laughing together so much, in memory of what people call misfortune, that must be the gift of being siblings, the gift of being brother and sister.

~

That's what I said to myself, but I made sure not to say it to him, it's what I said to myself, just for me, just to myself while he was laughing, while my little brother was laughing as he raised his bandaged index finger because laughing triggered the pain, and then his gesture triggered our laughter again, after all it was pretty impressive, three choppers for a finger.

Marie is the last one I pick up, and the first one to deliver the fresh and juicy rumour about my brother.

Adèle, is it true that you know Axel? How do you know him? Do you really have the same surname as him? Was he your husband? My mother said he hadn't been back for ten years.

They all start on it, intermingling the rumours with their various adolescent worries.

Yeah, he never worked around here. Apparently he even refused jobs on the plateau worksites, because his mother drowned in the reservoir. No, you idiot, she died before then. But still, after the flood barrier, that's when they brought in the wind turbines.

The older kids start having a go at each other about the turbines, and here we go, they undo their seatbelts and stand up, some for, some against.

I stop the bus.

Marie and Marine stare at them, incredulous and amused, and a bit anxious because of the time. On my right, Nadège is smiling, bored. I look at her, she gestures to me to ignore them, but I can't drive when they don't have their seatbelts on.

Teenage boys in the early morning, in an argument laden with adult pretensions, geopolitical analysis. They defend their territory.

The lakes are artificial, but not all of them, the flood barriers are narrow, the gorges long and straight and the mountains oval and shapely. The plateau is really long, the wind turbines huge, but how many girls are there in the area?

Julien is angry, his Adam's apple is going up and down. He's standing up, facing Joël. I find their battles tiring, they go back a long way, to the old days, well before the flood barrier. Girls have always been able to head off elsewhere and invent new topographies for themselves.

~

With the same anxious movement, Marine and Marie look at their watches, but the boys, ambushed by my silence, go and sit down.

I start the motor again cautiously, because the snow is coming down, it's really coming down, and now I can scarcely see the strip carved out by the snow plough's bow thruster anymore, although I know it is not far in front.

In the glare of the headlights, the colours of the trees are weird. The fog is stubborn, as if the night-time snow and wind was not enough. I cannot see a thing; it seems like all the bad weather has converged here since the wind started up again, and yet I have to keep going. And the kids are making a drama out of it. Marie asks me why there's no winter detour. Is it because of the landslide? If they don't want us to go on the road down below, do you think there's going to be a landslide there too? Will the snow be cleared from the pass? Why don't they build the tunnel?

I turn around to her. Trust me, calm down, we're following the snow plough.

If they start talking about the tunnel I'm really going to lose it.

The tunnel and the wolves, that's what they argue about the most. I hear Sébastien asking if anyone has a spade, and Nadège saying that by the time they find out anything about my life, Nielle will have grown a beard and Sylvain will be out of his hoodie. Sylvain replies, Yeah, that'll be the day we find out why that guy on the road came back when school started, and why we haven't seen him since.

(on the way to the primary school)

The snow stopped and the wind dropped, I couldn't even say when, just like that, during my break, and so gradually that I didn't notice. In the dawn, blocks of sunlight land on the cliffs, above the gorges. It's a sunrise that resembles a sunset, and I can get a good look at things before I head to the farm gates and have to tackle nervous mothers.

The witch never accompanies Lise and Minuit. For safety reasons, I am forbidden to drive to their house, even along the dry road. The children walk the two kilometres to the road, which is more or less clear of snow. They wait for me at the foot of the hill, like their big brother does. Lise told me last year that when the fog is so thick that she has to watch out for the snow on the ground, or when the snowstorm is too wild, she steps in her brother's footprints all the way to the bus stop, so that she doesn't get lost. And Minuit walks in my footsteps, but holding onto my coat.

My brother and I loved finding footprints in the snow. Especially ones that were a few days old. On some late mornings, the softened snow trickled into the hollows. By evening that water was frozen, but not at the bottom, only in the middle of the footprints, where it turned into a thin strip of ice, a transparent hymen that I took time and a huge amount of pleasure to rupture with new footsteps.

Lise buckles in Minuit and scoots to the back to sit in the sun. The route we take is full of bends, but it's horizontal almost all the way, and more or less follows the opposite direction from the sun. Towards the west in the morning, towards the east in the evening, well, not exactly, it depends on the season, but this morning, in mid-November, my route does correspond to the principle of heading away from the sun at pick-up time for the little kids. Lise looks out the back window, basks in the sunrise, and as she's almost a redhead, she is engulfed by the light. This afternoon, she will place herself in the sunset in the same way, in the soupy sunlight, and her face will glow red, then her cheeks will lose their lustre while I return the children to their homes. Right now the sun is hitting the rear-vision mirror, I can't look at it.

We're following the European Watershed. It's funny, the sky and the earth seem to have a dividing line between them too: in front of us the murky grey of the night, and behind us sickeningly bright colours. And by twisting around trying to see every-thing, Lise is going to end up vomiting for sure.

I drive round the mountain to pick up Thierry, Nielle's little brother. The sun changes sides, then settles once again on Lise's skin. Thierry sits down next to her and makes a face. We lose the sun briefly as we descend a bit for a few kilometres, and as we ascend again it is no longer rising but already caught in the blades of the wind turbines. I reach for my sunglasses as I greet two brothers, Tom (Year Three) and Bruno (Year One). They climb on board and show me the spiderwebbed snowflakes unravelling in their hands, laughing at the play of light on the tiniest sprigs.

The snow poles are garlanded with goatees of ice from a succession of days of windy, freezing fog. After all the recent anxiety about the weather forecast, it's frustrating: there are just these stupid toupees around orange posts, and a few remarks from the mothers.

God, it was terrible during milking this morning.

And you didn't have too much of a hard time picking up the big kids in this weather?

God, it was terrible.

When I used to be frightened of the dark, a darkness that seemed denser because of the tide pool around the farm, and when I didn't want to go and tie up the dogs or empty the compost (it was on my list of chores), my mother used to say: Go on, be brave, you have to scare the darkness, and then you won't be frightened anymore. So I stepped out into the night, making threats, but in the middle of summer the air was thick and seething with things that moved. The dark-blue flowers of the gentian plants filled the darkness, they seemed far too alive to me, they fluttered and that was it, I was too frightened. I tore back home, with no idea where I had dropped the bucket of compost.

This morning I was calm. I haven't been frightened of the dark for a long time, what's more I prefer night-time snow to daytime snow, it's less arrogant. I drive in the snow, the wind, the rain, the fog or the sunshine. In the cold it's sometimes a strain on the engine, but I brave the elements, as they say, and the mothers are in awe of me.

It's really stupid and irresponsible, but one day I'd like to be caught up in a natural disaster like my brother was, in an accident on the mountain. I'd like to be trapped inside a huge storm, a snowstorm in which the bus broke down and emergency services had to be called, the whole shebang.

The twins Paule and Nil climb in, silent and sullen, welded together.

Driving is easy. Beneath the chassis I hear the dull, reassuring crunching of the freshly scattered pozzolanic ash.

The gusts of wind have left outlines of shapes in the fields, in some places bumpy diagonal lines on the road, but there are no real snowdrifts before we reach the school. Just a busy trip, my mind focused on the children, on the pick-ups, no wandering thoughts.

Monday,
5th December

(on the way to the high school)

Nadège says hello, looking at me from below, her face contorted in an exaggerated smile. I say hello back. She sits down next to Sylvain and continues to stare at me. I sigh, she looks away. I wonder if it's that obvious. Yesterday, when I went to see my brother at his place, in the town below, he looked at me oddly, in the same way, from below.

I met a guy in the village square on Saturday, we barely spoke, except to say hello, goodbye, so I have no idea what Nadège or my brother could possibly interpret from my face.

What's the matter? I said to my brother yesterday.

Nothing, nothing at all. Nothing, he repeated, smiling, before changing the topic.

What? I wanted to slap him.

Nothing, Adèle, I didn't say anything.

I start the engine again in a bad mood. I'm worried about Axel, nothing to do every day, apart from going to the physio. I'm frightened that he won't be able to manage by himself. I made him a few little meals for the week. I will go and visit him next weekend if the roads are clear, it takes at least two hours on dry roads, so who knows at the moment. He's not used to looking after himself, he was almost never home, he went from construction site to construction site. When I arrived yesterday, I was shocked at how bleak his apartment was. I asked him to come and stay at my place, but he replied with the irrefutable argument that the only place he could see the specialist physio was down in town.

I'm worried, but I can't stop thinking about the guy, the hunter, and feeling absurdly happy.

On Saturday, around five or six o'clock, I was in the square, on my way back from getting bread, a heavy Briard loaf, still warm from the baker's second batch. It was my end-of-the-day time, when

I felt syrupy and warm, and I saw him, standing there, smiling. He wasn't like the others. Night was drawing in. He was leaning against one of the pick-up trucks, away from the group. I knew they had all come back from the hunt—deer or wild boar, I have no idea, I couldn't care less—they were noisy, idiotic as usual. If he hadn't had an orange vest and that annoyingly cocky stance, I would have sworn that he wasn't one of them, because hunters don't turn me on at all.

Nadège tries to persuade Sylvain to lift up his hood a bit and then whispers something into his neck. I really wonder which of them she'll end up choosing. Joël pretends to have his mind on other things, and Nielle acts as if she has never been of any interest to him, but it's impossible. All of a sudden I get the sinking feeling that I too am in the same situation, in love so much it's hurting me, like when I was fifteen, in love like an adolescent, with a jerk of a hunter.

He studied me for a while, I think, before saying hello, and I gave a confusing response. That happens to me often when I pre-empt questions. I assume, for example, that a person is going to say good evening to me, so I say thank you and to you too, and it sounds stupid, because the person said see you tomorrow. I don't remember what I said to him that missed the mark on Saturday, but I do know that whatever I said fell flat and he laughed. His laugh was attractive, and so was he in his orange vest.

Just thinking about him makes driving very uncomfortable. And last night's snow is getting on my nerves. I'd much rather go via the gorges, even though they're off limits. I know there's access before eight, after five, and on the weekend there are even minivans that use those roads, I passed a few yesterday when I went to see my brother, so why can't my little vehicle get through? The weather is so mild and overcast today that if it ends up raining on the snow, it will be like a skating rink. At least in the gorges it's less slippery.

I have another problem with greetings: I never know what time to start with the good evenings, I invariably launch into them too early or too late. If I run into someone in the afternoon, I always make a mistake, and the person responds with good afternoon or good evening—whichever one I didn't say. Perhaps that's what happened on Saturday.

Here we go, it's raining, what did I say. Oh boy, you're in a bad mood today, Adèle…And it's going to be sludge everywhere now.

Tomorrow, if the cold weather returns, all this snow swollen with water will freeze, we'll be able to walk on it without snowshoes, and the sound of it cracking will be really loud.

In the meantime, it's sludge, like in spring.

They say there's no spring here, it's just more snow during longer days. I think spring comes in obscure ways, in the unexpected mild spells of autumn, in the cold snaps of summer. The range in temperatures is more and more frequent, the severe droughts weaken the rocks, the fluctuations in freezing and thawing produce movement in the soil, the traffic on the roads intensifies the vibrations, the mountain is collapsing, and as well as all that, we don't even know what to wear anymore.

I should have been disgusted by him in his orange vest. I don't like hunters, even though I know the hunts are necessary, and I wouldn't take part in one myself. Around here, the hunters even take the trouble to knock on doors in the evening, on remote farms, in order to warn people that they'll be there at dawn the next day, and the whole morning, on the edge of the forest, or in so-and-so's field, we're telling you for the kids' sake, they say. I can't stand weapons, and I don't like the men's smug, self-satisfied expressions, and he looked just like that, full of it.

I walked past, right next to him, he said good afternoon (or good evening) as, with a resounding *whomp*, he heaved a tarpaulin over an enormous carcass in the back of a pick-up. Thinking about it now, it was probably too bulky to be a wild boar or a deer. I wonder if young stags pass through the shooting area occasionally, when the hunters are taking off their vests and diving into the forest.

It's really all just off-white mud now. I told the Year Nine kids to shut up so that I could concentrate on my driving, as if their negotiations over a SIM card were the source of my irritation. I'm so hopeless, too full of his laughter, his voice, his gestures, to ignore the brute. It was nothing at all (how long—not even a minute or two), but the memory of it is clenched inside my belly and my scars contract, they're almost completely taut. I picture him hitching his gun over his shoulder in slow motion. My scars trace the shape of my outer labia and they've been sensitive for ten years whenever desire makes them contract, not painful, but more sensitive than the labia of normal girls. I feel like an eternal convalescent, a new patient.

I gained a great deal of composure from the post-operative treatments. They took up two or three hours of every day in all. I performed the tasks patiently, I felt inordinately relaxed. I tried not to touch my clitoris—a bit of the head of the penis that had been retained and provided with a nerve supply. It was so intensely sensitive that I could scarcely stand putting on jeans. The dilation exercises with surgical dildos were pretty unpleasant, but at the physio I met a young mother with whom

I became friendly, and I enjoyed catching up with her there. I told her all about my second birth. Without any embarrassment, she told me about her failed episiotomy, her anger, her problems bonding with the baby, the useless father, the anxious older brother, all the endless postnatal worries. I caught her drawing little sketches. She blushed and shut her notebook quickly. One day she confessed to me that she wanted to write a novel, but that it always turned into a cartoon without speech bubbles. I've lost my words, she said. It was as if she had forgotten where she'd put them: I can't find my words. She cried when I told her my story, I told her everything, she was so natural, sweet, a brunette with pale skin, beautiful, sincere. I had the impression she was crying over her own story as she listened to mine. These intimate crying sessions were wonderfully good for both of us.

The rain is getting heavier, but I'm back on the highway, where the snow plough has done a better job. I can't manage to separate a slight feeling of guilt, resurfacing from who knows where within me, from a sort of intense excitability, a heightened sensibility from another era, a backwards era when we were burdened with just as much suffering and just as many emotions, but when the conventions of the day forbade talking about them, to the point that young women would faint at the slightest physical sensation on their bare skin. I feel as if I am disappearing, like them, into my scars and their poisonous contractions, as I remember the sound of the tarpaulin being pulled down over a pathetic good afternoon or good evening.

No, it wasn't pathetic, because he looked at me for a long time, because the reverberation of the tarpaulin is still pulsing through my thighs. And that reverberation makes me feel once again as if I don't fit into my body, like when I was an adolescent, as if my skin was too tight.

Yesterday Axel was speaking too loudly, but I didn't dare ask him to lower his voice. In the past he's refused to speak to me, and since his accident I've become his confidante, so yesterday, when he smiled his odd, idiotic smile, I pretended I wasn't looking, and when he started talking too loudly, I said nothing. I didn't want to risk another silence of several months or several years simply because I really hate it when people yell.

All he could do was yell when, after a period or two of silence and vociferous letters, he came to see me, to harass me. Harassing me was his way of dissuading me from having the operation.

He had come back to the apartment without warning one afternoon just before I left for Brussels—even though I had written to him to say that I didn't want to see him. I was frightened of him. I had warned my boyfriend at the time, who was standing by, ready to intervene if I telephoned him. My brother and I had not seen each other or talked on the phone for over a year. He would write me epic letters that made me feel completely insignificant, that reduced me to a state of pure, raw, unbearable pain. And yet I read them all, I inflicted on myself the reading of those long letters that arrived at regular intervals. They hurt me a lot, and yet sometimes they made me laugh, like when he rewrote the history of psychiatry to suit his argument. He wanted to put me into a box that suited his case a bit better. In some of his letters, he tried to get me to admit that I was a repressed homosexual, he found it impossible to separate identity and sexuality. When he wrote that—You're a homo—I tried to imagine myself sleeping with a girl, which just confused me. Then I understood that he had completely missed the point: he pictured me sleeping with a boy, even though I already had such beautiful breasts, and the body language that goes with them.

The evening before my operation, he was fidgeting in the twilight around my little suitcase, which was sitting on the couch. He was begging me not to go ahead with it. He was preoccupied with his own life and his memories, locked into his useless reasoning, he talked about how Papa no longer recognised us, and how he wanted still to be able to recognise me. And yet he was the one who had never tried to understand me, to know who I really was.

I looked at him as if he was abandoning me.

The operation that was about to happen was aggravating a discord between us that had existed forever, a vague misunderstanding, the echoes of which I nevertheless heard as a residual whirring sound that, even now, after all this time, hurts me, terrifies me.

Our adolescence had not gone well, and not simply because of Maman's death and Papa's negligence. Things had not gone well between us. Adolescence drove us apart. I wanted to speak about my body that I hated so much, I couldn't, so I stayed silent. He played the tough guy and that totally froze me out, it left me mute, helpless, deaf even when he tried to question me. I was terrified, paralysed by the fear of not being understood, and I think he suffered as a result of my silence.

That night he talked, and talked. He harassed me for almost ten hours. I had to sleep before catching the train. I was no longer listening, I was certain I had lost my brother a long, long time ago, I loved him so much, I loved someone who had disappeared.

If you do this, I won't have a big brother anymore, he said.

Are you listening? I wanted to do this job so I could be alone, do you understand, be inaccessible, yes, that's it, inaccessible, because when you are three hundred metres up in the air no one comes and hangs around you. But they keep tabs on you, from a distance, through binoculars. You can't see them. That other guy was looking at us through binoculars and he knew what was going to happen. Well, no. Well, yes. You know, I've already had discussions with guys like him, I often talk to them, I need to understand what they're making me do. I want to know everything, all the time, why, for example, is it only the wind from the south that knocks all those small stones down into the gorges, and how do they sweep the much bigger ones along in their wake? But those guys, not one of them goes up the mountain, not one. They take their photos from down below, or from a chopper, they stick them in their computers, do their little calculations, mark up anchor points. Well, a few points—the reinforcement points for the rockfall netting. As for the anchor points and the stud bolts, all the gear for the men to access the mountains, they don't always provide that, in fact hardly ever, especially when it's impossible to climb via the top of the mountain—that would be far too demanding for them. Here you go: printouts, diagrams, photocopies in the site logbook, you'll figure it out. I only knew one geologist who was also a rope-access technician, he worked out his anchor points directly on the rock. But all the others just look at you through binoculars. In their research departments it's worse, they don't have a broad enough perspective, they scribble away, five cubic metres to be excavated here, ten to be buttressed there, whereas the whole slab is like fifty metres wide—they don't notice the little crack on the left, they don't see the connection between that and the instability of the slab, and do you know why? Because they're not hanging face to face with it, because they're not alone, in the cold, in the gusts of wind—when you're not even sure if the rope is running through the anchor ring. When you're worried about the lifeline you rigged up for yourself. Sometimes, you end up in places where no one has ever been before, do you understand that? The site managers are the worst, they're just sales staff, selling their site, that's all. The foreman wasn't there and the other day, this little jerk, a young guy, he couldn't be arsed, he wanted to save some time and energy, and there you go.

What are you talking about, Axel? What on earth are you talking about? Because, right now, for me, what happened the other day doesn't matter. It's dramatic, but it doesn't matter.

Last year we lost a guy, it was fucking stupid, he got himself wiped out by a deluge of boulders, he passed under a full netting because he couldn't be arsed going around, can you believe it? Yeah, sure, okay, it's got nothing to do with the geologist, but when I record the eight-millimetre gap in the site logbook, he just laughs, it doesn't make him evacuate the area. He picks up his binoculars again as if we were just birds.

Axel lowered his voice, he seemed exhausted, he stared at me, sullen because I was smiling, but I was so happy to be listening to him, and I found it strange to imagine my brother roped up, observed through binoculars by some kind of boss who was a bit of a voyeur, a bit of a caretaker, a bit of an ornithologist.

He was bare-chested, he looked magnificent. It was the first time I'd seen his upper thighs since the summer of the burning tree. The summer of our departure from the farm.

~

When we were adolescents, I was disturbed by his body, sometimes I even despised him for it. After he'd come back from the barn one evening, he pulled off his shirt in front of the fireplace. He leaned forward, as if about to fall into the flames, warming his shoulders as his skin-tight T-shirt' stretched out of shape. He stuck his face further into the orange blaze and the back of his neck was exposed. I couldn't stand watching him, seeing what I was going to become, what I should already have been (Papa used to joke about the delay in my physical development). I remember getting up to set the table and pushing him aside as I walked past.

In the evening on the farm I always said goodnight to him when his back was turned, and I avoided turning over to face his bed. I never went into the bathroom at the same time as him.

I didn't want to get used to his man's body.

When I was finally ready to do it, in town, when I finally had mine, my body, he was the one who became fiercely prudish.

In our apartment, he would come out of the bedroom, throw me a bra I'd left there, and say,

For fuck's sake, don't leave your dirty clothes lying around.

In boarding school, we were never in the same bedroom, and I dreaded the weekends and the holidays because of that childhood bedroom we shared.

During high school, we had other things to worry about. Papa was forgetting things. The more he forgot, the more Maman came back to us, because we remembered then that she wasn't there. My body had developed, but I was determined to reject that body, so I stayed skinny, a daydreamer, as if I was in another world. We were more and more preoccupied by the memories of Maman that surfaced from Papa's forgetting. We talked about it in secret. We hardly ever went back to the farm. I had almost given up my habit of distancing myself from Axel's body, my panicky compulsion of remaining withdrawn, until the day his body reappeared before me—ablaze.

During that final summer, as the waters rose, just before we moved into our apartment, we wanted to have a party, a barbeque in front of the house, on the shore of the emerging lake. I had so many things to celebrate, some sad, some not so sad.

My baccalaureate, our departure for the city, and what we discreetly referred to as Papa's solution, a situation we were handling with kid gloves. We should have said the solution for Papa, but he had to remain the father, the one who made the decision, so we preferred saying Papa's solution.

Along with some friends, a few distant neighbours and Papa, we had set ourselves up around trestle tables near the water—the rising, rippling water where we liked to dabble our toes.

Papa went inside to bed quite early, as soon as the night set in. He told us to be careful with the barbeque, because in his opinion it was too close to the dead tree. And as the dead tree was against the house, and the house was not yet under water, he didn't want to see it going up in flames. Yeah, yeah, Papa, we're big kids now. We were just ribbing him, but he didn't seem very impressed.

My brother got drunk with the others. We let the embers die down. They all decided to sleep there, in sleeping bags, by the shifting edge of the water. I joked about their bodies washing up tomorrow. I sat absentmindedly watching lines of ants leaving a crack in the dead tree, then I went up to our bedroom. I felt a little uneasy in bed, and suddenly it hit me what the ants were doing. I ran outside.

The flames were already as high as Papa's face, as he stood there in his pyjamas, motionless, helpless. I sent him back to bed and I went over to wake Axel. He hurtled out of his sleeping bag, stumbled into his jeans, yelling at me to go and get an axe, quickly. The others stirred, but they were far too drunk, useless and tangled up in their bags. They went back to sleep.

I had already uncoiled a hose, but all I was doing was dampening the flames, through which I could see Papa shaking his head in the window of his bedroom. There was only a preposterously thin trickle of water coming out of the hose, the ground-water catchment was almost dry. I started carrying buckets of water from the lake. My brother, who was trying to kick the trunk of the tree, yelled out again: Stop fooling around and get me the fucking axe!

He began attacking the tree with the axe and there was his body, looming right in front of my eyes.

I watched Axel's shoulders heaving with the effort, his arms tensed. I watched the sparks at the end of his hands as they gripped the axe stuck in the charred flesh of the bark. I loved his firm arms, the colours straining under the skin. I heard the creaking of burning wood fibres as they tore apart. I loved the nape of his neck, the spot where the contractions of his muscles were firing. I watched as his sweat sputtered and sparks landed on his dark, glowing torso.

And then everything stopped, and with a weary kick my brother rolled the smouldering trunk along the ground to the water. The splattering and the sizzling woke up the others, who were soaked, startled, almost angry.

Yesterday in the hospital while he was talking, I was able to follow the shapes he made as he moved. His muscles are long and rounded. He has a labourer's muscles, not muscles from working out in a gym, and I find that touching.

You know, he said, in order to be a rope-access technician, it's not enough to be able to scale mountains and have confidence in your equipment, the anchor bolts tightened properly and all that, you have to have a hell of a lot of experience of the cold, of solitude, you have to be in peak physical condition. It's not enough just to know how to climb, you have to have confidence in yourself and know your limits, and work—work on your limits, your weaknesses.

He was whispering, as if he was delivering secret information. As I studied his arm, his forearm, his taut wrists and his good hand, I felt as if I was dreaming about his manoeuvres on the rock walls. But he sat down abruptly and hid his head in his magnificent arms, his words muffled, his hands grasping his hair, the splint raised above the middle of his head.

He was looking at me through binoculars, he saw the rock face detach, he watched me fall.

It's over, Axel.

No. The noise, you can't imagine the noise it made, the pandemonium, and all around every-thing was shaking.

I arrive at the village and the high school looms up ahead, perched on the hill, with a panoramic view from the boarding school.

~

My big kids grab their bags reluctantly. They still spare me a few words, like they always have. See you later, Adèle, have a good day, things like that.

I think yesterday was the day my brother came back to me.

Tuesday,
3rd January

(on the way to the primary school)

For a few days now, the good weather has refuelled the conversations. It's good for winter tourism, cross-country skiing, skating, telemarking, skijoring. And the plateau is vast beneath the sun, artificially vast. The beautiful, immense barrenness of winter. The rock walls appear even steeper and more picturesque. In my mind, however, the plateau is never as seriously soul-stirring as in a snowstorm or in the fog: the plateau, our roads, our fields, our forests and our lakes, our volcanoes. Our footsteps muddied and dripping in the sunken paths. Our footsteps obstructed by the wind. The wire fencing at the edge of the summer pastures catches hold of the droplets of water in the fog. I'd rather they were swallowed up by a snowstorm than sucked dry in a flash by good weather.

I don't like snow in the sunshine. It offends me. It's nothing more than a tourist attraction, just there to dazzle.

The weather is extremely cold. Faint stars float in the air, wispy stars made of ice, tiny, living stars that fall onto the snow. Minuscule transparent spiders. It looks like the most incredible, sparkling translation of a Christmas carol.

Hugues is playing around with his boots, I can see him bobbing up and down in the distance, and when he lets go of his mother's hand he leaps into the bus at full speed. He tries to explain to me as clearly as possible (except that he can't, he's too excited) how the snow today doesn't seem to be the same as usual, if I understand him correctly, there's a funny kind of frost on top, and it looks exactly, exactly, exactly (he pronounces that word perfectly, three times) the same as the grated coconut on the New Year's Eve cake the day before yesterday. It's like the snow has changed, like there wasn't even any snow last night, and I just wanted to eat it, but my brothers and my sister, they say that you can't because the snow, it's like a filter. But I really want to…He stops to gasp for breath, and to put on his seatbelt like a big kid, next to Minuit, then the two of them start up again with their quirky kids' chatter about the weather. Lise keeps an eye on them from a distance.

Hugues' words fitted exactly with my feelings. Despite the difficulty he had articulating them, he used words of terrifying precision to describe my loathing for this violently beautiful weather. When it's fine, it's like the sickening taste of a birthday cake, or a special occasion, which impels us to go out walking in groups. Walking with family, with lovers. You have that bad taste in your mouth, but you've got to hold hands, and smile, and say how lucky we are, oh yes, I think we can agree that things have turned out well (especially if you're on holidays, what a splendid day it is).

~

I drive past the watershed between the Atlantic and Mediterranean oceans, two arrows on a signpost in a picture-postcard landscape. Shit, it drives me crazy. Bring on the evening.

Paule and Nil climb on board in a bad mood.

Non-identical twins, brother and sister.

They were born here, swaddled in their parents' unfortunate reputation as tree-huggers. Roughnecks from somewhere else, carting around weird habits and ideas about outdoor education for the people. The neighbours still occasionally poke fun at their composting toilets: almost like back in the old days, when people shat in the cowshed, remember, their turds sprinkled with sawdust, or hay in the summer and dead leaves in autumn, it's disgusting. The twins say they throw their mandarin peel in there too, and their hair after Maman has cut it. Papa says it all turns into compost afterwards. At least we aren't wasting drinking water on shit. The others shrug: what difference does it make, since the runoff from the groundwater catchment overflows alongside the farms.

There's no shortage of water.

The twins' problem is not the smell of the dunny. It's the sound of the wolf.

You can still hear it years later.

Soon after the birth of the little ones, the roughneck father took into his care another set of twins, Shendo and Dryad. A male and a female wolf. It was all illegal. He put them in the care of the leader of the dog pack, a big Siberian husky, and they immediately fell into line. The guy had gone to a zoo at night and taken the twins, in order to demystify the fear of wolves propagated by human stupidity: I'm telling you, hunters and also writers, storytellers, yes, the ones who wrote Little Red Riding Hood, they're all complete idiots, even stupider than the cops. A wolf is like a caver's rope, it allows you to go deeper, to arouse the spirit, do you get it, to damn well throw light on all those narrow-minded ideas, yeah, those idiotic fables. That's how the roughneck talks.

I like him.

When he was bottle-feeding them, he would hold the wolf cubs right up close against his body, so they could smell him, as he told them all about the fucking human race.

They didn't gulp down water, they lapped it like dogs. Shendo was already holding his tail in the air whenever he went near Nil. With a big clumsy paw, Dryad begged for pats on her tummy, and Paule would sprawl on her belly.

But the wolf—not a wolf holding its tail erect, not one of their wolves—had been spotted early one morning, near their house, in front of the bus stop.

The tracks of a large deer ahead of the wolf's tracks meant there was no doubt about it. The wolf was on the prowl, otherwise it would never have come so close to the hamlet, wild wolves are too fearful. And a pet wolf would never have bothered to chase a deer.

The reactions to this apparition were extreme and contradictory. The hunters and the tree-huggers came to blows, while Nil and Paule tried to keep up at school.

The trouble started one Friday morning around seven-thirty, right at pick-up time, as I was arriving. Ten police officers and four federal wildlife officers with poles and syringes turned up to remove the wolf-cub twins.

My twins were crying over their favourite puppies. I managed to get them into the bus, without attempting to comfort them. I know children are inconsolable at that age. I felt ashamed, sitting in my bus not knowing what to do or what to say. The other children kept quiet, we all kept quiet together.

But a few days later the wolf was still loitering, dragging its tail through the mist on the plateau, its fur no doubt barely ruffled by the rumours or the dew.

The controversy took on surreal proportions, my kids recounted fairytales and old-wives' tales their parents had twisted in the telling. We were off in the realm of White Lady legends, and our crazy guy on the road, who had been eaten by the wolf, or else just the sight of the wolf, yes, when the guy saw the wolf it unhinged him. Paule and Nil wouldn't stop crying.

Their exasperated teacher tried to tell them a different version of the fairytales.

He told the school council, and all us adults, that he was going to lodge a complaint with the public prosecutor about the graffiti on the stone wall that borders the road through the gorges, because, being clearly visible in a public place, it constituted a provocation to racial hatred.

Some idiot had written, in large capital letters, like in kindergarten, DOWN WITH ARABS, HOMOS, JEWS, COMMUNISTS, GREENIES, WOLVES, BEARS.

So Nil and Paule kept sniffling.

In the beginning, Tony didn't want us to see each other in the village for fear of gossip. He told me about a hotel in town. No, actually he didn't tell me about it, he took me down there one weekend: he pulled me by the arm and sat me in his pick-up truck. We didn't say a word the whole way. He parked, we got on a tram and headed to the first cheap hotel we could find.

I was embarrassed about going to a hotel, but I would have agreed to anything to be with him. It was raining. Raining nonstop, and in our room there was a picture of a rainy scene stuck on the ledge above the bathtub. In hotels there are always paintings that are not real paintings, just decorative knick-knacks. And there were plenty of tacky paintings in this hotel. In the bathroom, however, it was different: the painting seemed to serve no purpose other than to be itself, the image, the texture, the rain. It was beautiful, a single plane, blocked out in blue. There were people standing waiting, scarcely visible, umbrellas swallowing their silhouettes from the shoulders up. They were on the margin of the picture, as if reduced to the outer limit of the figurative form, and only the blue rain, blue, blue and grey, emerged clearly at the surface of the painting. The canvas was simply stapled onto a flimsy stretcher. It was not particularly hygienic, I wondered how the cleaning woman dealt with it. I imagined her lifting the picture up quickly, giving it a wipe with the sponge, then putting it down again. I stayed in the bath, curled up on my side, my face up against the painting, contemplating it sadly, listening to Tony moving around in the bedroom, as if he were a long way away.

I put on a dressing gown and went to join him, my vision filled with blue, blue, blue and grey. He turned around. I'd never felt such a powerful urge within me, and yet I didn't want to make love in the hotel, and not right then. I lied to him and told him I had my period, trying in all honesty, or as a game, or I don't know what, to imagine what sort of pain it would be, uterine contractions and sharp pain all the way down my back. He said it was no big deal, and I didn't know what that meant—if he wanted to fuck anyway, or if not fucking was no big deal. I suggested that we go for a walk in the rain. I said I liked the rain, even in town, and that it would help me to put my abdominal cramps out of my mind.

I got dressed quickly. Since my operation, I no longer wear make-up, and I've given up the corsets (but I do wear tight-fitting bras, otherwise I don't feel good).

As we were walking towards the town centre in the rain, wandering around, I ended up getting stomach cramps—those sort of cramps—for the first time. It was exactly what I thought it was, and it was for the first time, but I knew this pain from somewhere. I tried to persuade myself that it was impossible. I didn't have a uterus, ovaries or fallopian tubes, and yet I could feel a fistful of flesh writhing inside me above my vagina, with a regularity that felt both relentless and excessive.

I was experiencing pain in that unthinkable spot. I was experiencing pain in an organ I didn't have. And I was bleeding. I was aware of the blood. I was bleeding without shedding a drop.

In the throes of a contraction, I remembered having felt pain like that, as strong as that, when I was still a little boy, well before I had the operation, but sometimes things happened, hardly anything actually, a flash, a few words, certain films or stories, things that overwhelmed me because of Maman. I was watching some stupid movie on television, for example, and something made me think of Maman's miscarriages. I didn't really know what it was, but I got stomach cramps. I wondered if it was because I was already a girl that the flow of memories of my mother's miscarriages was so heavy and regular.

I found unexpected answers to my speculations, and I re-remembered private conversations between Maman and Grand-mère, who had also had countless miscarriages, and no doubt her mother before her.

From within that pain I knew that not having a child was what it meant to be a woman. It's not about having a child. To be a mother is to lose a child, to carry a burial vault where brothers and sisters will be clinging on. I felt pain right there, with a raw, violent awareness, I felt pain in that cavity that was a mortuary, the cavity that belonged to my mother, where I come from.

Apparently, in the past, it wasn't the same, they just slipped out. I know that's not true, I know that's just bullshit spouted by historians, clichés people repeat, in order to keep going, to deny the truth. Grand-mère lost three children to whom she had already given birth, one of which was stillborn, another died as an adult. Grand-mère cried easily, but through her tears she maintained that she also suffered a lot with the others, perhaps even more so. The others were all the ones who never made it to full-term, whose fragile cords were snipped with a fingernail, and whose features were often only hinted at in an outline on a body, those who had one.

We went into a café because the rain was coming down in sheets, almost solid. I was certain my brother had never had abdominal cramps.

If I had been born a girl, I would already have

got pregnant. I would already have lost those scraps of foetuses, tiny, minuscule, but sometimes already so well formed that the eyelids flickered, the lips quivered, ever so precisely, just below the surface, on the verge of taking shape.

Tony said, Hey, what are you thinking about? You look so sad. I vowed to myself that, one day, one evening, I would tell him everything.

I sleep with him amid secrets. The village secret, the secret between us, but also the secret of myself, that I have never shared with anyone, except Axel.

(on the way back from the primary school)

All the beautiful sunshine has disappeared behind the clouds.

I'm happy being with Tony. He is still cautious when he comes to my place. He stays silent, as if to talk would be to risk getting caught. We don't do anything bad, but whatever. He gets undressed in silence in the bed, so carefully that the cold flows into his movements. When he pulls his T-shirt up over his shoulders, his torso makes the sheets whisper and billow, and I shiver.

Below the wind turbines, right at the spot in the landscape where the artificial lake appears, treeless in my memory, I see something in the mountains. The clouds depositing their mist all the way to the ground are not thick enough to block my vision, even in the distance, but in some places they obscure the transparency of things, while in others places they enhance it. Right opposite me, right opposite us, sunlight is filtering through a rectangle of vapour, yes, an almost perfect rectangle. I wouldn't call it a filter like, I don't know, a water filtration system by the sea, for example. No, it's like one of those filters you screw onto the lenses of old cameras to alter colours. In a rectangular frame of landscape, all the colours have changed, but only inside the frame. It's the first time I've witnessed a poetic weather event with the children. Lise says to me: Look! But the preschool children, standing up in a group together, are all worked up, like tablets fizzing in water, which spoils everything.

The twins are still in a bad mood. They've been carrying on some big quarrel, just the two of them, since this morning. The reason for the quarrel will remain a secret, just like everything that doesn't concern others—that is, everyone else, even their friends, their parents. Their sibling bond is stellar: an evening star twinned with the morning star.

They are both night stars, but do not shine at the same time. They are different and inhabit the same sky, a sky that no one can see, and where no one can be admitted. In the bus they're arguing about some place or other in that black sky. Because we've stopped in front of that other sky, the landscape in front of us, they've used the opportunity to leap up like the preschoolers and attack each other more vehemently with their insults. They're unbearable. And yet they're nine years old. Every day they swap personality traits, physical quirks, until we're all confused. I think that's precisely what they're after. They're non-identical twins who seem more identical than identical twins, non-identical and of the opposite sex, but possessing one mind, one set of responses, along with strangely androgynous games, wrongly cast, violent games, which I find shocking, and which in particular, against all the odds, always fail to demonstrate any evidence of a difference in gender. Their favourite game is to pretend to kill each other. I wonder what will happen when Paule develops the body language and curves Lise has, that all girls have. Right now she's grabbing her brother around the neck. Nil says to me: But Adèle,

155

we're playing. They're unbearable. And as soon as you reprimand them, they close ranks, inseparable. We've fallen into their trap: we refer to them as a pair, the twins, or the children, we almost never call them Paule and Nil. I understand why their parents raised wolves: it must have been soothing for them.

Meanwhile, Hugues, Minuit, Bruno and even Tom are having the time of their lives, playing annoying games extremely loudly. Thierry and Lise are keeping quiet, the only ones to give me a bit of a break.

When they grasp their children, by the arm or the hand (depending on the age) as they get off the bus, the mothers tell me that it's always worse an hour later. If you only knew, you have no idea about that witching hour between six and eight o'clock, when they're hyper. Well, you don't know *yet*, Hugues' mother says to me, so that I'll understand she already knows about Tony and me. Nice of her.

Around here a proper couple is bound to have children.

(on the way to the high school, by myself)

When I think about that mother's words, the subtle nod and a wink, I realise that the complicity inherent in what she said has shattered my confidence. I don't want a child—that's not the problem. But I lie to people, I lie to my own life, my life itself is a lie, and if Tony finds out, and if everyone finds out, I'll have to go away, Tony will leave me, exile will be like a punishment.

I try to stay calm by making the most of this space I'm in now, all by myself, in the silence, which will last until the big kids arrive. But I can't. I don't have space inside myself, only the echo of the excited little kids, like a permanent, inexorable ringing in my mind. I'm no longer able to shake off the reverberations of my kids.

They always work my uncertainties over. I can't think when I'm with them.

They are my noise, my life, my lie.

(my break)

I'm waiting near the high school for the big kids, in
the car park, leaning against the wire fence, eating a
mandarin. Shards of ice have broken off the nearby
roofs and are crashing next to me. I jump every time
it happens. It feels warm beneath the clouds, as if
they had retained and cossetted the day's sunshine,
whereas during the day it had been so cold out
under the clear sky. I throw the peel through the
fence into the ditch.

My place is on the ground floor. You enter from
the street, there's a sort of lobby area where you
take your shoes off, like at school (around here you
put slippers on to go into class), and further back is
the kitchen, which looks out on a small courtyard,
closed off by a wire fence. Behind the wire fence is

the park, which I can also see from the window of my bedroom on the first floor (the bathroom and toilet face onto the street). I live in a council house, there are a few of them, all the same, in a row. On Saturday and Sunday, and on Wednesday afternoon when there's no school, I can hear and see all the village kids, the ones who don't take the bus. They know me anyway, they say hello, and so do their parents. Some evenings, and even some nights, well after the park's closing time, I see the kids from the high school, and on the weekend it's older kids from the high schools down below. I don't say a word when they clatter their beers and talk too loudly, but my neighbours sometimes complain. Some Saturdays, I see my big kids from the bus. I have no idea how they manage to get there, they must organise a lift with an older guy from high school, or a big sister. They drink and flirt gently, they laugh, even when it's snowing (but not hard).

Especially during the thaw you can hear them.

They were often there during the Christmas holidays this year, because the weather wasn't that cold. Nadège was there late one night, I wasn't sure who she was kissing (I don't know the guy—he was around eighteen or twenty, I reckon). I could see very clearly under the full-moon blue sky, magnified by the snow. I didn't want to be a stickybeak, so I closed my shutters. It was almost midnight. When I opened the window to close the shutters, Nadège startled like a little flurry of snow, before saying good evening to me, her laughter heightened by being caught off-guard so stupidly (she knows perfectly well that I live here). She was also a bit drunk. Because of the beers, because of her youth, because of the phosphorescent snow, because of that translucent blue of our nights. Behind the shutters, I remembered what I'd heard recently on the news about the curfew imposed on the outskirts of Paris. I realised that Nadège was probably not even fifteen and that, if she had been living there, she could have got herself arrested by the police, dobbed in by one of my neighbours, just for an evening of tipsy kissing in the moonlight. I also caught sight of something else, but I couldn't quite work out what exactly—a detail I'd noticed about Nadège. But whereabouts on her had I glimpsed it? And what was it?

161

Tony was asleep, incognito (as if) in the bedroom. I went upstairs and lay down next to him. I felt all the more in love with him knowing that down below, right near us, Nadège was experiencing her life of hugs and kisses, of flutters of excitement in her belly. It was nothing to do with voyeurism or some kind of perversion, no, it was just that, once again, I had the out-of-sync feeling of being the same age as her.

Nadège comes up and leans against the wire fence. She asks me what I'm dreaming about. I reply, no, no, I was thinking. About who? About you. Oh, really. She climbs in the bus, I follow her, she takes off her scarf, goes and sits up the back. I sit down behind the wheel. The others file in. Then I stand up, head down to Nadège and ask her to lift up her hair. She sighs as if I'm going to tell her off, but she does as I say. Almost in the middle of the nape of her neck, at the hairline, there's a tiny tattoo, the little detail I had noticed the other evening. She's got to be kidding. I'm a bit worried about her. Last year she got a piercing in her lower lip. It didn't heal properly and no one dared to make fun of her:

162

we all felt sorry for how disgusting it was to look at her with her infected mouth, unable to smile. Her parents, who had not been in favour of the piercing, were almost happy about the result. I was appalled to see Nadège all swollen, withdrawn and punished in such a painful way. The tattoo is not too bad, but I thought you had to be over eighteen to get one. And I wonder under what circumstances she bent over, bowed her head and offered up her nape. I also wonder if her parents know about it.

The others all want to see it. Nadège refuses, acts like a celebrity, plays the innocent, then changes her mind, stands up and leans over to reveal her little bug to the boys and to Marie. I tell her to sit back down because it's time to leave. What Nadège did by showing her tattoo to everyone was to hide from them the importance and mystery of that little bug, a type of potato beetle that is climbing up her head. And I'm intrigued, because I've seen that same silly mark everywhere, on benches in the park next to my place, and also on the back of road signs, on doors in the village, discreetly drawn above a seat in the bus (on the edge of a window) and even on one of the security fences on the construction site in the gorges. I can't fathom the insect's itinerary.

I hope she knows what she's doing, that foolish girl.

(on the way back from the high school)

I change the radio station, they won't be happy, but I need to hear something else. I turn off the musical compromise that normally accompanies our time together. We settled on this compromise years ago: neither a young people's station nor an oldies' station, instead we either have silence or tune in to a local community radio station with a broad musical program, but no crap, no young people's crap, no oldies' crap. I come across a classical music station. They object. I let their little protest flair up then die down. I need to turn things over in my head. Think about my life, about Nadège's life, the path I'm on, the one she's on, about my past as an adolescent, about her future as an adult.

I don't manage to think, but at least I clear my vision a bit while listening to this music.

For no apparent reason, the music fades, stops, starts up again. In clearing my vision, I've lost sight of the road a bit, but, in the empty field of my thoughts, I end up, despite myself, venturing a glance back at my big kids. I see them in the rear-vision mirror, next to me, everywhere. They're not playing up, no one is speaking, almost no one is moving. They seem intent on something I'm not aware of. An authoritative voice is talking over the music. A man's voice repeated, or rather dubbed, inside a false echo. Eventually, I grasp that it's the voice of an annoyed conductor, a foreign and unfathomable voice, using everyday words, dubbed in two dimensions and in French, another man's language. The conductor's tantrum is being transmitted in a simultaneous translation, but his angry tone is not being duplicated, the translator's words fall flat; there is no texture to his voice. The two voices overlap each other, one full of intonation, perhaps in Polish, the other monotone, in our language. Too short, too short, says the second voice, translating. Too short, again. Both voices are silent, the music swells. Nielle seems fascinated. The music dies down again, no doubt in response to some invisible signal. The Polish conductor launches into his outburst again, chastened by French words. These discordances, this impossible mingling, this muffling of the music, is both annoying and thrilling. Because of the music, the conductor is silencing the musicians. The conductor deadens the music for the sake of the music. Because, as the other voice tells us in dubbing, the music does not exist as long as it is like that. He holds it back so that it can come forth. The language he speaks is strange, made up of unusual words, a musical vocabulary that is beyond us. But we understand what is happening, what is not happening. We can almost hear the terrified and respectful musicians, breathing as imperceptibly as possible. We're holding our breaths too. The music picks up again. The conductor gives it one last whack with his silent baton. And the big kids and I snap out of our strange hypnosis and burst out laughing. And the music finally finds its place, within our laughter, and no longer fades out. It swells, powerful, an expansive sweep that carries our laughter along with it.

I saw the potato beetle on the security fencing when I went down into town to see my brother. As if on some sort of unconscious pilgrimage, I had stopped near the construction site, which was closed on the weekend. I wanted to see the site of the accident, I wanted to cry. I walked along the fence, without having a clue where my brother had landed. I remembered the other landslide of five years ago. I had a particular memory of the flowers left by the family of the guy crushed inside his car. Still wrapped in plastic, they were stuck in a crack between the rocks, and no one dared to move them. They remained there for several months, getting rained on, then snowed on, ageing faster than the rock. After remembering that, of course I thought about the guy on the side of the road, our crazy guy. I thought about the way he always looked surprised, and I thought about all the stupid stuff the kids said about the White Lady. The White Lady stories made me think about the blue cows. I looked in the other direction, and they were still there. It was so beautiful, everything was so good, and I was proud to be from this place, with all the crackpots on the plateau.

In the spot usually reserved for signs warning tourists about the risk of pickpockets, there's a sign alerting people to the cows: Herd of Cows—Beware! It's the normal triangular shape, except it's clearly not a professional sign and a white cow with blue stripes is poking out of the triangle. When you look over where the sign is pointing to, on the other side of the road, in the middle of the cliffs overlooking the gorges, there are blue cows, roped together, their heads angled into the fold of the rocks, their large wooden bodies jammed into horizontal crevices, and decorated with stripes, or love hearts, or flowers. The primary-school teacher got the kids to make them last year for the Pansy

Flower Fete. The kids couldn't stop telling me about it for weeks (Mine's the cow with the love hearts, Mine's the one with the stripes, etc.), and when their teacher abseiled down to wedge them into the gorges, they were so proud of their cows and of their teacher. And therefore I was proud of my kids.

Years before that, a Citroën 2 CV that had been sawn in half was cemented directly onto the vertical rock face. It loomed out from the escarpment into thin air. We all pretended not to know who could possibly have conceived of a thing like that. We all pretended to believe it had nothing to do with the tunnel project.

I was smiling as I returned to my car. I had completely forgotten my brother's accident. I'd parked up against the security fencing and it was as I got into the car that I noticed Nadège's little creature (I didn't know then that it was hers). I'd already seen it in the village, in the bus, and thought it must have been a sort of tag, a tag used by one of my kids, but, hey, nothing more than that. A kind of harmless, funny signature, and so much less vulgar than the inscription in capital letters on the stone wall up the mountain.

I continued further down memory lane as I drove, to a morning last year, in October, when my Loire kids and I headed along the lower road in the valley, past the mountain.

There was a construction site there as well. I've known about reinforcement structures forever. There are people around here who are the great-great-great-grandchildren of men who came from Italy to build the roads through the gorges using the system of roping up the workers. They were often badly roped together and many died during these impressive construction works that took place, who knows, at least two centuries ago.

We were following the security fence, all day-dreaming as I drove, just as I was now. It was dawn on a hot, windy Indian summer's day. The lulling motion of my driving was disturbed: I braked suddenly and Sylvain popped out of his hoodie. Five or six fenceposts were lying on the road in front of us. I turned round to Nielle and Sylvain and they got up at the same time. You could smell the wind outside. It was the smell of summer in autumn. The weather was mild, incredibly gentle, and that's what they were too, incredibly gentle in the way they moved and in the way they remained quiet. We picked up the fenceposts without saying a word to each other, apart from laughing a bit. It was hard work, and yet it was easy. It took us a good quarter of an hour, alone in the dawn wind. I was helping them or they were helping me, I don't know which. What I do l know is that I felt safe with them.

Friday,
17th February

(on the way to the high school)

Beneath the corbelling along the road through the gorges, stalactites of broken ice are lying in messy piles on the ground. I have to weave around them. The guys from the Department of Environmental Management are still shooting them down with rifles. They haven't cleared the ground, so I pull over while they finish blasting the ice, the noise of the gunshots made even louder by the echoes. They wave me through, and Sébastien and Julien turn around in their seats to watch them reload.

Rifles are customary around here, part of the landscape, what with hunting and the biathlon of cross-country skiing and shooting. For me, it's out of the question, I'm not the slightest bit interested.

175

Nadège sighs. Marie and Marine look down the gorge as they take their seats again. They had stood up in order to see even further down, their hands on the window, their eyes staring, trying through the half-light to make out the depths of the steep rock faces. Sébastien and Julien are swapping stories about the next shooting match in the stadium not far from here (in a huge clearing set up for the world championships).

It's reassuring to see Sylvain back under his hoodie and Joël and Nielle asleep, daydreaming at first light—so sport and firearms are not simply a gender-related thing.

One morning three weeks ago, Tony took me hunting. I said yes to getting up early, to walking through the night next to him. I said yes to please him, because he was keen, because I trusted him, because walking less than a metre from him made my stomach gurgle (still does), and the snow would mask that, all crunchy and hard at dawn in the forest.

I said yes so I could release the low pine branches stuck under the snow and, like when I was a little boy, enjoy the sudden wet slap as they sprang up. So that, simply by the absence of undergrowth, I could locate the old paths—forest paths that are thinned out at eye level. So I could walk out there where the trees no longer grow because of age-old footsteps in the ground. I said yes so I could walk on the scarcely forgotten footsteps of others. My brother and I had a game we used to play: we'd look for paths that had been all but entirely forgotten, old municipal roads between abandoned hamlets, places that only old people have names for now.

I said yes because it was the last Sunday of the hunting season, and it was clear that he wanted to mark the occasion, somehow make our relationship official (the words used by Hugues' mother, now that they had done the rounds on the plateau). I said yes because by now everyone knew I was going out with Tony, and Tony is not just anyone, he's one of a kind, both loathed and adored.

Farmers offer him a coffee or a glass of red, hoping to negotiate the price of their meat. He replies that he can't give them more, I mean perhaps for a bull but not for a cow. Oh, you've got to be kidding, who do you think we are, eh? All this time we've been doing business together, Tony, the females are worth as much as the males. Not that one. What do you mean, not that one? She's a real beauty. How dare you say she's not a beauty. The debates are endless, the woman of the house hangs back, her backside against the sink, and only comes over to fill up the glasses again. Do you want this cheque? Tony says. No, not under those conditions.

I laugh when Tony imitates the accent of the old people—so familiar to me—mixed with his own—he's from mountain country, but not from around here (and that's another thing to hold against him). Otherwise, Tony is a volunteer fire-fighter. Respect!

I said yes to this wordless outing in the forest because I like his voice, I like his accent, I like what he says, but I also like his silence. I said yes because he describes to me so often and so well the patient focus needed and the tracking of the animals' emotions on the bark of the trees, that scent they leave clinging there, sometimes made more notice-able by a few hairs left as well. I said yes so he'd explain to me all those tracks in the snow, often mingled with my kids' footprints.

When they climb into the bus, they know perfectly well if they've stepped on and rubbed out the tracks of a wild boar on the run, or a hesitant deer—they tell me (as their news item of the day). White snow, virgin snow: that only exists in books.

I said yes so I could hear our footsteps crunch, fall silent when we stopped walking, then start up again, and so I could focus on one of my favourite silly ideas: the notion of being followed by things— when branches, tree trunks, frozen bushes, all the things from the winter forest set forth with us, and at any slight break in our rhythm come to a halt, almost after we do.

Invisible shooters shattered the stillness. That ruined it for me. Tony smiled every time I flinched. He held me in his arms until I buried my head in his shoulders. Hunting is really not your thing, is it? Do you want to go home?

(on the way to the primary school)

The day is blue enough to loosen the creases in the sky. The weather is so beautiful and so cold that the air seems to be cracked in places. It looks impenetrable. But we'll soon have to drive into it.

The cold even seems intensified in the sunshine. At the big kids' pick-up time, it was minus seventeen, and I'm numb enough to feel that the temperature is dropping.

I can't grasp why I'm feeling so anxious in this blinding brightness. I can see the road, and I'm used to the cold. And yet I seem to have lost my way, or my memory of places, or perhaps of the pick-up schedules.

180

~

Last year in April, I'm not sure how I managed to do
it, but somehow we got ahead of the snow plough,
and we arrived in front of some huge snowdrifts. I
was with the little kids, we were warm inside the
piles of snow, the sun was already high in the sky.
We had almost reached the village, the school, but
I was feeling happy-go-lucky and decided not to
wait for the snow plough. I parked the bus a bit
further away, so it wouldn't block the road, but
was still clearly visible (so they'd work out we were
here). The kids were thrilled to walk the rest of the
way, to climb up and down, up and down, on the
mounds of snow. Sometimes the snowdrifts joined
together two fields normally separated by the road.
Sometimes they had stopped disgorging snow and
it had stopped cascading in waves from the drifts
and was left suspended in the air, which created
tunnels underneath, gaps the size of Minuit and
Hugues, who disappeared inside, then jumped out
shouting peekaboo at us.

But even during the fun I was filled with
anxiety—nothing at all to do with the possibility
of the snow plough suddenly appearing (you can

181

hear it coming from a long way away, and see the powder spurting). The kids were running around like crazy things, like animals held in captivity for a long time and then released, like winter calves the day they leave the stable for the first time once the thaw begins. They were crazy and beautiful, all red-faced in their scruffy snowsuits, I loved them so much, but I was unexpectedly terrified, to the point of being unable to smile.

We heard the plough, so we headed off to school and arrived via the field at the back. (Y'know, Adèle, the little kids said, there are donkeys here in summer and autumn, and they go *hi-han* while the teacher's talking.)

My paralysing terror disappeared once I thought about the donkeys, but I still didn't know what had triggered it. I only understood once I was on the way back from the school, returning on foot, alone, along the freshly ploughed road. It was simply because a few hundred metres of the road had been closed for a few hours, because there hadn't been a road there anymore. My extreme anxiety was due to the brute physical shock of the devastating and yet harmless loss of my bearings, of my route, of my trip, of my particular spatial habits.

Today I feel the same anxiety, and yet everything is in the right place: the road, the cold, the mountain, my memory.

I stop to pick up Thierry. He's all red in the face and smiling. Hmm, he doesn't sit next to Lise.

I try to drive smoothly, so that the oil doesn't freeze and flakes of ice don't get into the motor. I should have put a bit more petrol in there.

After the wind turbines I slow down to speak to the kids. I want to be sure that the little ones have lots of cream on their cheeks. The big kids check on them, and on the kids from Years Five and Six. Yep, all's good, okay. At twenty degrees and below, delicate skin can get frostbitten, and it's not just red cheeks, but full-on, extremely painful haematomas. Lise points out to me, kindly, but she says it nevertheless, that mothers, even her own, know all about frostbite, and about undergloves and snow-boot socks, they're on it. I apologise; Sorry, I say,

I don't know why, but today I'm frightened of the cold.

The wind rises, stirs up the snow and hides the sun. It gusts under the bus, bears down on the windows, buffets us a bit. It settles almost immediately.

The road seems longer than usual, but it's not. Time seems to be slowing down, but it isn't.

I know that, if there's a high wind, the snow plough will come and bore into the snowdrifts, and this time I'll wait for it.

I don't trust the sun today, everything seems artificial.

Today is the last day of school before the winter holidays.

I've already been forced to take detours in the past because of the fog, when even the lights of the wind turbines couldn't penetrate the darkness. I've never panicked before, so I try to get a grip on myself: we're all tired in the lead-up to the holidays. I'm battling the feeling of being in some banal and childish dream in which the road goes on forever and I make no headway. The snow is good, firm in the cold. But the road is so long, and the school is so far away.

Back in the day, as we say, there were lots of schools. They were more or less everywhere. We all still walked a fair way to get to school, but not all in the same direction.

Back in the day, or rather back in my neck of the woods, before the artificial lakes and shuttle buses, we used to arrange with the neighbours to go to school by tractor whenever there was a snowstorm. But the schools were nearby, none further than ten kilometres, whereas I travel a good twenty with my little kids, and still more with the big kids. Schools used to be part of the landscape, just like farms, scattered around, dotted here and there. Each village, each hamlet had its own school, but there was no need for a village or a hamlet to justify a school's existence. If you visualised a circle containing three farms or ten houses, spread out over the mountainside, you would be bound to find the school in the middle, on a road. Some of the schools constituted official localities in themselves and had their own name.

Mine was called Bertoire. All you could see from Bertoire was the mountain, and a bit further down the road a house where some old people made bread, which they sold to the schoolteacher. The teacher lived above the classroom. She had enrolled her daughters in order to prevent the school closure that was forecast every year. I don't think she even knew where the students came from, but they turned up every morning, scarcely twelve of them, including her two daughters. There they were: the children from farms that were out of sight, two orphan girls from town who had been placed with some old farmers, three boys from a farm even further away, an only child born late to another couple of old farmers, and my brother and me.

There we were: standing outside the little gate. Behind it were two crooked staircases, opposite each other, which provided access to the school on the edge of the mountain. The teacher would come down to open the gate and check whether I was there (I was the only one who regularly didn't turn up). Some boys wore shorts even when it was snowing, their legs ruddy and swift on the stairs.

I liked going to school, but I was often sick, ill at ease with myself.

The teacher had improvised a sort of lunch room, not a regulation canteen or anything, but it was warm and convenient. We would go upstairs to her kitchen and reheat the food prepared by whichever parents, not just a snack for each set of siblings, no, it was a meal for all of us, prepared by each family in turn. By the teacher as well, since her two daughters were there too. As there were five families and no school on Wednesday, no family ever got the same day of the week, but we knew the schedule by heart. We would start whingeing first thing in the morning when it was so-and-so's meal day, with their disgusting soup or whatever it was, or someone else's stew with gristly pork-and-greens meatballs. Anyway, we whinged the whole time, except the days when it was our parents' turn. We whinged for the sake of whingeing, because, if I can remember correctly, I think the food was good every day.

What was downright unfair were the jobs of setting and clearing the table and sweeping the floor, because the boys had to do it more often, on the pretext that we didn't know how to do it, so we had to learn, we had to attain the same domestic standard as the girls (our teacher was a bit feminist). I was often let off the hook because I knew how to do those chores (they were on Maman's list). So the boys mocked me, telling me I should have been born a girl, and for a while I got a kick out of telling them that one day I'd be a proper girl. All that carry-on meant that we had a good time in the lunch room, because that's where we argued, we stood our ground, we got angry, but all in good spirits.

My brother and I always fought about the girl who was an only child. Her parents and our parents had come to an arrangement for the driving and Maman used to pick her up on the side of the road, where the path led out from her farm. By then, she'd already walked a couple of kilometres in the forest, but even the scent of the undergrowth that I loved so much did nothing to change the fact that she smelled bad, as if she'd been born too late, as if she was too lonely, as if she had been lost in the forest for a long time before reaching the road. We used to fight about not sitting in the middle, next to her, and when I think about it now I feel a bit ashamed.

Bertoire closed down, it got turned into someone's holiday house. The farms around were also sold, others were overrun by vegetation.

The branches of the trees are growing over the paths, all over the run-down buildings.

The forest is taking over the vacant land, and land ownership is dwindling, despite farmers having access to wood from the local municipal forests. Our paths are disappearing beneath the mass of trees as dark as night, and the perfumed obstinacy of the shrubs.

I don't know what's happening to me. I feel overwhelmed by nostalgia, a bitter, miserly nostalgia that is not attractive. I'm withdrawing into myself. I feel threatened, spied on, sidelined. I feel as bad as I did with my old body. But how can I feel bad in my own landscape? It's all nonsense.

~

My brother told me that small-scale mining creates weaknesses in the rock—the work renders it unstable—and yet it has to be done in order to re-inforce the rock. He told me that bolstering the cliffs only results in delaying or more or less controlling the collapse, because monitoring everything would take too much time. They work like crazy for months, a year, on the same slab, and then the restrictions on the regional budget compound their exhaustion. In any case, all the corbelling is going to fall down for sure, but we don't know when, it's going to happen in the years to come, since some of it has already given way.

And, he told me, you know very well that the roads were all built at the same time. Forget the geological fault mapping, the presence or absence of parallel sedimentary stratum, the layers of soft clay behind—none of that makes much difference. Yeah, okay, it helps, but it's only going to delay or precipitate the collapse.

He also said that it is often financially easier—those were his words, financially easier—and faster, to rig up a rope and rock climbing route, to install footbridges in caves, to secure the rocks above ski runs, than to maintain the roads I drive the bus along.

Gradually his words became more and more disheartening.

I have a very clear memory—piercing, painful and inexplicable—of the reasoning behind the soundings they carried out on the rock walls in preparation for the future tunnel works. I can see the probe drilling a little hole ten centimetres in diameter, but driven fifty metres deep from the surface, in order to place sensors in the core to ascertain whether the rock moves during the explosions and shots of the tests. He told me that, whether you like it or not, they have to have some idea of the stability of the rock mass, and he laughed at how hurt and upset I was about the holes drilled into the mountain.

When I think about that scene, I miss my brother. It's been a while since I went down to visit him. Tony doesn't much like it when I go and see Axel. We argue about it a lot.

~

I feel as if the local land management is keeping me at a distance. Quite honestly, I feel removed, but removed from what I don't really know. From my home, perhaps. Isolated from things, as if I had no name, or no voice, no legs. I feel as if I'm no longer connected to the spirit of the mountain.

When they wanted to install the wind turbines, they assured us that up there would be perfect. There was no one there, only the wind.

I arrive at school without a hitch, and all day long I try to persuade myself that my fear was just as meaningless and stupid as the expression on the face of our crazy guy by the side of the road.

(on the way to the high school, by myself)

My stubborn fear takes hold of me again. The wind has picked up, gusting continuously, a blast from the south, a blast from the north, like a giant slap from nowhere. Again, it rises from within objects and inside people. It dislodges the snow and another sort of snow falls over the top—dry, ashy and light. The temperature is around minus twenty, it shouldn't be snowing. I think the snow is being carried from far away by the squalls from the south.

This snow isn't from around here, it comes all the way up the mountain and piles on top of our snow. You can see it leaving the gorges in colossal waves, as high as the sky.

~

When I reach the wind turbines, I notice that the snow—that is, the wind—is now contained in a horizontal band, raised above the ground at approximately the height of the bus. Down at the level of the tyres and my footprints (I got out to check because it seemed so strange), there was nothing up to about calf level, and nothing above the roof either.

There's only one remaining snowstorm area, as tall as a man, as if the bad weather was demarcated, framed (in a three-quarter shot), and within this frame there is our space, our road, our life. A snowstorm just for us, from the knees up.

As I park at the high school, I request instructions on the two-way radio. I don't feel up to recrossing the plateau. The school boarding house could put my kids up for the night, since the boarders have already left and gone down the mountain to take their trains and buses. Too bad if the staff have also left, the principal's still there, and if worse comes to worst, surely we can find a few families in the village, one or two kids could stay at my place. We managed to find ways of getting the boarders home last year when the school supervisors went on strike.

The reply on the radio is no, the boarding house is not an option, the holidays have begun. The snow-cutters have already started to drill into the biggest snowdrifts, I have nothing to worry about.

(on the way back from the high school)

If I have nothing to worry about, well, let's get going, I've seen worse. I park and leave the motor running. It hits me hard when I open the door.

They're waiting for me, huddled together against the wire fence, whether to feel less cold or to feel connected, I'm not sure. If I'm a bit late when they come out of school, I often find my teenagers like that: clustered together, a single body, tighter than a gang. Even Sylvain is in among them, even Nielle.

The group dissolves as they get in the bus. Sylvain emerges from his hoodie to ask me if it isn't a bit risky, after all. I shrug to say that I have no idea, and that it's out of my hands.

He puts his hoodie back on and shouts: Here we go on a big adventure.

Sébastien chimes in: Did you bring the spades this time?

I've got the spades, and a head torch. If it takes us three hours, I have an electric torch, but no candle.

Ah, Adèle, that's really not good, because a candle...a candle (he hesitates) guarantees the temperature of the passenger compartment stays above zero.

I have space blankets.

The Year Nines did an orienteering course today, so that means we have two Swiss Army knives.

In the snow?

Yes, he's a lunatic, that teacher. Adèle, you've no idea how many teachers are lunatics. So, yeah, we also have two Swiss Army knives. (They show them to me.)

Nadège says, Stop, you guys, that's enough, we're not in a reality TV show. Sorry about them, Adèle, they're still into cowboy games, you know, they've got all the gear.

~

I smile, but it's because I'm thinking about a night I spent with Tony when there was a power cut. We were about to go to bed, he had put on his head torch to go and find something in the kitchen. I told him he looked handsome with his extra eye. He replied, Wait, you haven't seen anything yet, and proceeded to do a clumsy striptease, an awesome striptease in the light of his head torch.

Nadège is right. The older boys also have their head torches in their pockets. They bring them out when she says the word gear. And she brings out hers, admitting with a smile, yes, but a head torch is not the same thing: at my place we don't have any street lights outside, well, there isn't even a street. Julien then gets out his mobile phone. And don't you have the two-way radio, Adèle? Driver, we're ready.

With a sense of team spirit, they've all tied their head torches around their beanies (and Sylvain around his hoodie). I love them. But they mustn't forget to fasten their seatbelts as well.

The game's over now, we're lost and neither my radio nor the mobile phones have any reception. We're not completely lost, I can tell—and I know—that we're not far from the volcano, the lake, my lake, where I take my break, but I can't drive any further in this snowstorm.

I turn on the warning lights. I look at Sylvain and Joël, sitting up front next to me. The others have withdrawn. They still have their head torches on.

I don't know what to do.

I don't know at what point the parents or the emergency services will start to worry, I don't know if they'll find us, I don't know if it's wise to wait with the bus, the nearest farm must only be five or six kilometres away, perhaps fewer, but I'm incapable of working out exactly where it is.

The kids aren't sure what to do either, they all have different opinions. We really can't see far at all. The whirling snow is like a screen of shifting dust, dust bound together, as if lashed by the wind—we can't see through it and neither the headlights nor the emergency lights can penetrate it. I might just be able to feel my way down to the lake, among the trees, following the hollowed-out rim of the volcano.

That shadow down there, that's the trees, the forest around the lake.

Are you sure, Adèle?

Yes.

But even if you made it to the lake, and say you got a fire going on the beach, how does that help us? We're no better off, Adèle, we might as well stay in the bus, we have enough heating for a few hours.

I don't know, we're probably down to a quarter of a tank.

Sylvain scratches his hoodie.

I look over at him, and whisper directly at him: Or else there's the cave.

He returns my gaze, laughing: The cave? Where the caretaker used to live?

Uh, yeah, the caretaker of the lake, the troglodyte. The cave we've been to a few times.

Sylvain continues my line of thought: You're right, it's sort of cozy inside, basic, but there's a fireplace, straw, the cow sculpture (he hoots with laughter). Then he recites: *The troglodyte caves were restored and opened to the public with the support of the local government, to enable visitors to engage in an intimate experience of the lives of the inhabitants who lived here until the end of the 1920s. The caves are man-made, dug out of the volcanic material that resulted from an explosion caused by the confluence of water and lava.*

Stop, Sylvain! Adèle, make him shut up.

The caves are testament to the highly innovative dwellings inside the surrounding volcanoes.

The others scream, Stop! Oblivious, Sylvain continues his annoying theatrical recitation.

Adèle, please, make him shut up.

On the ground floor, the old home of the caretaker of the lake has been reconstructed, and on the first floor an exhibition space has been created. My father is a tourist guide in Germany.

Yeah, sure (Sébastien hates Sylvain), and your mother the witch must know how to force open the door, although (he perks up) it should be fine if the wood isn't too wet, if it's not frozen stiff.

Joël isn't certain we'll be able to get in over the glass panel that runs the length of the corridor. Behind the panel the interior design and furniture have been reproduced for the tourists (or the visitors—sometimes the brochures use the term the public).

Of course we'll be able to get in, even Sébastien. We'll give the little kids a hand. At least we'll be warm while we wait for the rescue team. We'll be able to drink the lake water, we'll smash the ice, or we can drink snow, we'll melt it in a saucepan—yes, there are saucepans, they're hanging on the mantelpiece, they've put everything back the way it used to be in the olden days.

Sylvain just told you, Adèle, they've restored everything, to make it look authentic. Like it was back then.

Yes, that's right. Now, everyone, leave your bags here, only bring the bare essentials. Okay, iPods, yes, but especially your head torches. And snacks if you have them. Snowsuits too. Surely you wore them if you went on an orienteering course in the snow? So put them on. Snow boots as well. No one had ski class today? (No, it's the Year Eights on Friday.) Okay, come on, let's go. I'll bring the space blankets.

The older kids are smiling. They joke around as they watch Julien and Joël get into their snowsuits in between the seats. Your change room is not that convenient, Adèle.

Yeah, anyway we're going to do it again.

What?

Uh, the orienteering course.

All right, you can all laugh. I just hope the others have snow boots or proper walking shoes (I turn around, bend down to check). You're kidding…I can't believe they're wearing sneakers. Marie and Marine are anxious. I tell them to trust me.

We're going to leave a note under the windscreen wiper. We'll have to walk two or three kilometres, perhaps four. Two or three more if we come out on the other side of the lake. We'll head down through the forest, and I want us to stay together as a group. The snowstorm is raging up here, not so much among the trees, but I'm guessing there'll be fog down the bottom.

I stop and collect my thoughts.

Okay, everyone, when we get to the lake, we won't know exactly which side of the lake we're on, we'll continue on around the edge until we find the cave. In the forest, I want you all to gather firewood. Break branches if you have to, even though they'll be green. Oh no, they won't be—in winter the moisture recedes. I want each one of you to pick up as much kindling as possible. And if you have scrap paper in your schoolbags, that'll be useful as well.

Sébastien announces that he has plenty of class notes to burn, but what about logs of wood?

No, don't worry about wood. There must be half a cubic metre of wood next to the fireplace, to look authentic, as you said, like in the old days. I just hope the flue isn't too blocked.

Marine and Marie are rattled: we'll never be able to get this fire to shine.

Around here, that's what we say, shine the fire—we mix up light and heat, and it's fire after all that will allow us to see better in the cave.

Girls, listen to me, even if we can't light a fire, a cave stays at a constant temperature, it must be, I guess, about eight degrees at that altitude. It's the best solution. Come on, is everyone ready?

In the forest the fog is as dense as flesh, you can touch it. And, as we continue, we really don't know what we're going to touch, or what is going to hook onto us, apart from the tangible, freezing fog. The dark trees add their black backdrop, and my big kids have fallen silent out of respect mingled with fear.

All I can hear as we walk are their hollow footsteps, behind me, in front of me, the crackling of dry branches, the breaking of compacted snow, gusts of warm air, sometimes right next to us. The layers of snow are carrying us higher, towards the crown of the trees.

When the snow was high and the sky full of sunshine, my brother and I used to lie near the top of the young trees, beneath the forks of the lateral branches. Bands of sunlight fell through the shadows of the branches, and our faces would be sprinkled with crusts or crumbs of snow, depending on the strength of the wind.

The snow is hard, but every now and then the kids' legs disappear entirely: suddenly they're up to their thighs or hips in it (I hear bursts of laughter). We're close to the pinnacles, but also to the raised forest floor. The snow-covered ground is scribbled with pine needles and dust and pock-marked with frozen snowflakes. We walk hunched over through the undergrowth, where the snow has been dirtied by forest fragments dumped during weeks of head-winds. The torches illuminate the slightly perfumed terrain all around us.

And yet we move rather swiftly, but cautiously, into the space of a clearing, chalky-coloured and chaste, like a resting place.

In between the spindly trunks, the water is rising. My big kids start talking again, in anticipatory relief, and go back to being what they are, carefree, chatty and annoying. I take a break to do a silent headcount in the twilight of their torches.

We arrive at the edge of the lake. Silence descends on us all again, but it feels different now. The water is smooth, slick as a polished stone. Close to the shore, the waves have been clotted by the ice. No one tries to go out to play on it. It's not that my big kids, still children, don't want to play. They'd love to, I know. But the lake is a sinkhole with hundreds of metres of water in the middle, the sound of which you could hear by smashing the ice, thus breaking our silence. The frozen, sleek waves of ice are barely visible, covered by snow from the storm. When the wind gusts, you can glimpse the ice beneath the snow in places, because the wind that piles up the snow is the same wind that carries it away. Further away, frost flickers, blinking in a gap between the clouds and the snow. Even further away, you can intuit the movement of water starting up again in the middle of the lake, open like a dilated pupil.

~

I send the younger kids up to the head of our line. After scarcely five hundred metres we reach the beach. It's completely dark now, but the beach of snow and wind lights our way. The little path that leads up to the cave is at the other end. The boys muck around on the white beach, but I remind them that I need all their young male strength to force open the door. Their spirits are dampened by the thumping they're getting from the wind that has taken refuge in this exposed place.

Everyone cheered Sébastien. The door opened at his first push.

We made sure to close it again properly.

The inside of the cave is fitted out for tourists in a sort of long, narrow corridor. The window panes, set into solid aluminium, run along both sides and along the end, circumscribing a U-shaped display area. The tourists are meant to stay in the corridor, inside the U. On the left is the meal area, on the right the sleeping area, in between is the stable (the bottom of the U is taken up by a hay rack). The high windows are made of thick glass.

~

As we entered, our moving head torches cast a patchy glare on this place that we were used to seeing under neon lights bolted beneath the lower part of the window frames. It seemed weird, and no one said a word.

Julien and Sébastien gave Nadège a leg up first. She glided down the other side of the glass like a flower, all cold and wet. She had taken off her shoes so she could get a better grip with her right foot in Sébastien's hands and lever herself up with the other foot against the window, all the while laughing about how incredibly cold and ticklish the glass was. Julien held onto her hips, telling her she wasn't that heavy after all. The boys all tumbled over by themselves. Julien chucked over Nadège's shoes, then they took turns to jump up and grab onto the metal rim at the top, hoist themselves up using their arm strength and drop down the other side. (Move over, Nadège.) Nielle stayed with me so we could pass them the shivering little ones, who were frightened, fatigued, freezing, and in awe. They shrieked as if they were at the funfair.

When it was my turn, I took my boots off, threw them over, and Nielle lifted me up, then he climbed over by himself like the others.

I've managed to get the fire going without too much trouble. There was no shortage of lighters in their pockets, wet, but still working.

It's stupid, but we all really feel like we're part of the historical re-enactment, even though there's no one behind the glass to look at us.

Marie has noticed some half-decent clogs sitting on a makeshift bench.

Well, sure, I say to the kids, put them on. How many pairs are there?

We line up our shoes around the fireplace. There are enough clogs for all my big kids.

It doesn't matter about me, I'm fine in socks. No, don't worry.

Julien and Joël take off their snowsuits and go and hang them on the hay rack. I look at the others, drenched and exhausted.

I think we'll have to strip down to our underwear.

They all protest. I stand up, ignoring them. I make my way round the U, then hand out all the scraps of material I've found in the display furnishings to the boys, the sheets and bedspreads to the girls. So they can stay together, Marie and Marine pick a single sheet, made of stiff, coarse cotton, and leave me the other one. I send the boys off to change on the other side of the U, in the bedroom (just a small bed in a dark corner).

We girls are going to undress in front of the fire.

The three boys come back with cream-coloured scraps of cloths tied around their hips and forbid us from saying a word. I feel a bit foolish in my dusty sheet, so I don't say anything, and the little kids stifle their mice squeals behind their own sheet.

Holding her bedspread tightly shut around her, Nadège places a battered packet of cigarettes on the mantelpiece.

The boys' clothes dangle from the bed frame opposite. We hung ours on top of the windows. I feel a wave of sadness when I look at them drying.

~

Sylvain is leaning over Nadège, he takes her hand, lifts her up and asks her to follow him.

They are hidden behind the hay rack when we hear Nadège squeal with delight, then Sylvain leads his princess back: he has dug up a beautiful black-and-red dress from last century.

Yeah, Adèle, it was on the bed.

Probably a Sunday-best outfit. Looking drop-dead gorgeous, Nadège spins on her heels in her clogs, smiling and bowing. Her damp black hair glides down the flounces. We cheer for the second time.

Shh! says Sylvain to us all, pointing to the baby doll in the cradle next to the fireplace.

Joël has set himself down at the end of the table and, imitating Julien's grandfather, calls out to Nadège, demanding his dinner. He gets out his pocketknife, opens the blade and wipes it up and down on his scrap of cloth repeatedly, all the while swearing in a dialect mixed with rapper slang to annoy Sylvain. Marie, who has been holding back tears for a few hours, starts laughing (and crying a bit too).

~

The nine of us don't all fit around the table, but it's funny because we're wedged behind the window where our clothes are hanging. In order to make room and to compete with Joël, Julien goes and sits at the end of the cave, on the (contemporary) cow sculpture. In front of the wooden beast there's a sign advertising parsley-flavoured meat. We're definitely hungry, but we're already sharing what we have left in our pockets, and it will pass—I know and they know that we can go a fair while without eating.

The glass fogs up, we draw on it, and manage not to get bored. If I wasn't thinking about Tony, about the kids' parents, about their anxiety, if I didn't know that the kids were all thinking about it too, I would even feel quite okay.

Sylvain, who has just come back in from taking a piss, after putting on his clothes that were still stiff with ice, gives us a report on the night: The sky's clear, plenty of stars. (But I froze my arse off.) They're reflected on the frozen surface of the lake—the wind cleared away all the snow, it's really beautiful.

He clambers over the glass again to join us, and knocks over the cradle when he lands.

Nielle starts talking about the boarding-school mirage. Sébastien remembers it too. Last December, every night at the same time, the boarders got caught up in the mystery of a luminous spot in the schoolyard. It had nothing to do with the moon, or the streetlight, it wasn't a bit of something that reflected starlight onto the asphalt surface. Ten minutes every night at the same time.

Every morning they went out to check. There was nothing in the schoolyard.

Sylvain starts up again. I swear to God, Adèle, it's as cold as stone out there, not metal. The lake's like metal. He looks at me and in his eyes I see my lake, my break, crammed with lights.

They must have sent out a search party by now.

Julien asks me if it's true that Tony is a volunteer fireman. So perhaps he'll be the first one to find us. For sure.

Nadège asks if she can go outside for a smoke.

I say, Yes, but then bring back some snow, I'm thirsty.

Marine shrugs. Yeah, right, go and freeze your lips off.

Nadège doesn't bother teasing her. She could have smoked next to the fireplace. She picks up her packet of cigarettes, removes a few that might be smokeable. She takes off her clogs, gets a hand up to climb over the glass, grabs her clogs from Julien when he stands on the table to pass them over to her. Thank you.

Then the cooking pot, which I pass to Julien.

Shit, my lighter.

Sylvain picks it up and slides his hand between two metal window supports towards Nadège's hand. I notice his delicate wrists, his slender hands.

Their hands touch, indistinguishable, and their fingers briefly interlace.

Suddenly concerned, Sébastien is staring at Marine. He starts telling me about the cows' backsides. The calving season has begun. This morning, the vulvas of four of his cows were hanging out. The cows had lain down.

It had popped out, do you get it, the vulva was outside. Those vulvas have been puckered up, bulging outwards, for fifteen days, and the nerve has already snapped. Cows've got a nerve, you know, near the tail, up high. When it's time, it snaps, and makes a hole. I promised my father I'd help him this evening. Four at a time is tricky, and one of them was full of a big calf, perhaps two. I'm the one who gets them ready for caesareans, it's easy. I call the vet, and I shave the cow's flank. I don't know how my father will cope all by himself.

He seems to be pondering the situation, his forehead wrinkling like the backsides of his cows.

Who knows, perhaps they've calved during the day.

I pat his forehead with my cold hand. If you ask me, I don't think your father is that worried about the cows. They're going to find us, you know.

Now we're on for a round of gory stories about all sorts of freakish calving incidents. They trawl through their young memories for stories they've heard, carried down from their ancestors. I let them tell the stories, so that the wrinkles on their foreheads, the blood-stained bumps on their chapped and trembling lips, all their frown lines are transferred into the bovine vulvas and the blood-streaked buttock clefts, so that, instead of the tears they've held back, what flows are the tall tales of full discharges of afterbirth secretions onto the straw.

For now, it's about who can describe the most hardcore calving, while still remaining credible. Malformations, stillbirths, haemorrhages. Long, tough births (they compare size and breed). Prolapsed uteruses that have to be put back quickly by the vet thrusting his arm inside before the cow croaks.

Through the door she left ajar, I can see the quivering red of Nadège's third cigarette and the dark shadow of her arm, extended for over a hundred years.

I can just make out the overflowing pot of packed snow at her feet.

The caesarean stories are hitting the mark. It's Charolais country round here, the calves are large, larger than the Aubrac calves. Cutting open a cow is a common occurrence. The vet knows how to do it, but so do the farmers. Scarcely a week ago, a cow belonging to Marie's parents was cut open. Standing, the left flank slightly anaesthetised, she seemed to withstand the shock. But as they were finishing sewing her up, she collapsed, just like that, without a sound, except for the thump of her big, numbed body on the floor. All the stitches split open. She bled to death. Marie had to unwind the hose. She emphasises just how much water she ran in order to rinse the floor in the stifling warmth of the cowshed.

Julien starts another one, a legendary, decades-old story, but they shut him up: not that one, we know it already.

No, hang on, I don't, I insist, and they all start telling me, each with their own variations, their memories, their parents' versions. The story is twenty, twenty-five years, thirty years old.

You know, Adèle, the rope worker, Axel, it happened on his parents' farm, the bottom farm, right where the lake is now, the other lake. Oh yeah, of course, you know Axel. Well, that's where they found the cow. Alive. Alive a week after the first contractions, unbelievable. She'd been drinking from the river. There used to be a river there, down the bottom.

I know.

All the ground around the cow was flattened, trampled. The calves were dead. They say it really stank there. She'd gone into hiding. In the morning, the owner had worked out that she was due at midday, and then when he returned to the field, she'd gone. It's often like that, when they calve in summer. When they're not in a cowshed, they look for secret spots. The calves were still stuck inside her.

No, that's wrong, one was outside, one was inside.

You're an idiot, she'd pushed them out, both of them, otherwise she would have carked it.

Yeah, but anyway that's how they found her, by the stink of the dead calves.

I ask them if they're absolutely sure there were two calves.

Oh yes, twins. (They're all in agreement on that point.) And the cow was still alive. The vet said so, he said she had to be left outside. He gave her an injection to stop infections, and she survived. I'm not kidding, Adèle, she was alive.

Sylvain looks at them, a faintly scornful expression on his face, and announces that, on the subject of damaged vaginas, he has a much better story to tell us. Oh no, it's not at all what you think, it's beyond imagination, something you'd read about.

You should take your clothes off again to dry, I say. He does a little striptease for us, adjusts his scrap of material, then puts his jumper back on, and his hoodie—it's been a while.

Nadège comes back inside, the pot in her arms. From behind the glass, she tells him to shut the fuck up. Sylvain persists.

No, I mean it, she says.

You don't even know what I want to say, he counters.

She puts the pot down and holds out her arms. The five boys get up to help her. Sébastien and Julien leap over the glass to the other side to help her. She climbs up and lets herself fall into the arms of the other three boys. She stands, grabs her clogs and the pot that Julien is holding for her. Just like a mother from days of old, she hangs it on the hook near the fireplace, and slips into her clogs. Like a little girl, she neatens up her dress, smoothing the folds, then sits down next to me. She gives me a look that is both sly and eager.

You're the one with the frozen lips, Adèle, she says, you never speak about yourself, we don't know anything about you, except for Tony. But there's Axel, for example. Axel from the bottom farm, how do you know him? Why have you got the same name as him? Okay, sure, it's a common name around here, but still. And what about your life before you arrived here, all that?

Sylvain's eyes are like slits. His expression is still scornful, but now tinged with glee.

He stands up and takes Julien over to the other side of the panel to do a performance for us, or so it seems. They walk around until they reach the bedroom and press themselves up against the glass.

~

Now that Marie has delivered herself of her bloody story, she is crying silently, I mean crying her eyes out.

In an uncharacteristic gesture, Nielle puts his arms around her, gently making fun of her: Oh, she's crying for her mother. Come on, cheer up, they'll find your note, don't worry. It's awesome here, don't you think? Look!

He points to Julien and Sylvain opposite, leaning against the window, getting clobbered by the cold, making faces and squashing their distorted features against the glass, dribbling warm drool in some sort of private contest. Sylvain has kept his hoodie on, which makes his grimacing mouth look even more grotesque. Marie starts laughing again.

I wrapped Marine inside my sheet when her Siamese twin went and sat on Nielle's knee. I feel her warm body tense up when she falls asleep and wakes with a start straightaway. She drops off, stiffens, wakes up. I slide her head onto my shoulder.

Sleep if you want to.

No, not yet, I don't want to sleep yet.

I sympathise with her battle.

~

Nadège is looking at me closely. I finally reply: We should have brought a camera.

She gets out her mobile phone, as do the others, and Sylvain and Julien take ghastly pictures of everyone striking poses, then Nadège turns to me: Yeah, okay, so there you go. Now, let's get back to where we were.

I point out to her that no one knows anything about her potato beetle either.

You first.

Sylvain has come back to our side. He wipes his mouth and takes off his hoodie. Everyone whistles as if it is some kind of miracle. Swaggering like a movie star, he sits down, looking pleased with himself, and turns towards Nadège.

I know, he says. Axel is her brother.

All my kids gather round, arguing like they do about the White Lady, about landslides, about the guy on the side of the road, but they all agree on one thing: Axel did not have a sister, only a big brother. I tell them to be quiet. The condensation on the windows thickens, keeping the warmth in. I ask Sylvain to be quiet too, and then I say: No, go on, continue.

It's my mother who knows everything. That's normal, she's a witch.

And he begins to tell the story of my life.

He tells it as if he was summarising a book, as if he was talking about a film, bits missing, or made up, a bogus timeline, but almost everything is accurate.

I stay silent, stupefied, my head spinning, just like the others listening. When Sylvain finishes, no one dares speak. I want to slap him. I want to thank him. I don't know. It's done, I say to myself. Tony will be furious, he'll leave me. Yes, but it's done, everyone on the plateau will know who I am. I look at Sylvain. His expression is so serious, so calm.

In order to stop my tears becoming visible, and because he must have seen that soft, watery glistening in my gaze, a bit like the water moving beneath the ice on warmer days, he starts talking

again, joking, urging everyone to back him up:
Hey, I told you my story was good.

He turns to Nadège and reminds her that she promised to tell her story next.

She didn't promise anything, she retorts. Anyway, Adèle, Sylvain shouldn't have spoken for you, what he said doesn't count. Everyone lays into her, but she says, No, no way.

Sylvain puts his arm around my neck, assuring me that they're not all fascists on the plateau (with a wicked glance, he points at Sébastien and Julien). Besides, tomorrow you'll be everyone's heroine, the woman who had the idea of going down to the lake to turn her passengers into climate refugees, or I dunno, whatever line the journalists use. He gets all theatrical and pompous again. They're going to put it on the front page, the headline: *Teenage Troglodytes: Students saved by a school-bus driver*. Hey, Adèle, do you think they'll use the photos from our phones? Who knows, we might even get on TV.

~

Nadège is furious and tells him he's a stupid jerk. Did you even think about her boyfriend? Tony's like us, he probably doesn't know, he'll probably drop her now, you're a real pain in the arse.

Sylvain doesn't reply. He tugs his hoodie over his head again, then turns it inside out in a grand gesture, announcing solemnly: On the topic of the couple…He yanks at the fabric so we can all see the potato beetle, inked onto the inside of his hoodie, next to the label, near the back of his neck.

He stands up, heads over to get his jeans from the hay rack, and pulls something out of his pocket, a kind of applicator. He cleans the transparent partition with the back of his sleeve and sticks the object to it. He presses.

I haven't marked my territory here yet.

He detaches it and there's the little creature on the glass.

Or here, either.

He tattoos it onto the wooden table.

But I've already done it here.

He sweeps his hand under Nadège's hair. She tries half-heartedly to extricate herself.

Other guys can always put their big fat paws on her, but I've put my stamp on before them.

She consents without smiling, with a look that is closed, resigned, but staunchly, resolutely complicit.

The yawns are contagious. It's two in the morning. Julien walks around the glass case to reach the bedroom on the other side of the cave. He bends down opposite us and touches the bedspread. I signal to him: no. It's too wet and is probably mouldy. Through the two glass partitions, his back looks like a mirage. He returns, picks up the blanket Nadège has left, and rummages in the hayrack to salvage some dry hay mixed with local alpine fennel, smothered in dust. I lift the baby doll out of the cradle so I can get to the straw. I give the doll to Marine. Nobody makes fun of her.

We spread the hay and the straw out in the back of the cave, against the manger, and my kids go to sleep cuddling up to each other. (You have the bed, Adèle, it's for old people.)

I'm not going to sleep. I go back and sit down in the eating area and look across at them falling asleep. I don't know who is lying next to who. I'm not sure I can make out which are the little kids among the shadows of the big kids. I couldn't care less. There they are, in three heaps, near enough to both confuse me and reassure me. From a distance, the flames catch the silver and gold reflections of the space blankets, which crinkle with the slightest movement, and soon fall silent.

I turn back to the fire, I poke the embers to rekindle it a bit.

Nielle touches me on the shoulder.
    Not asleep? I say.
    He asks if he has to go to sleep.
    Of course not.
    Sylvain joins him. He's on edge, he says apologetically, in a low whisper.
    I ask him how his mother the witch knew anyway.

He smiles as he reminds me of what I should have understood.

There's no magic about it. My mother sat next to you at the physiotherapist's. She had those disgusting things done to her too, you know, with electrical probes, after she gave birth. She'd just had my sister, and already wanted to dump the father. We lived down the bottom, not far from the town. So she was alone again, like after she'd had me. She needed to talk. And there you were, you'd just had the operation. And you needed to talk too. She told me all about it, she told me your life story back then, I was four and I remember bits of it, because it was pretty weird.

Afterwards, we moved up here, to follow my mother's new boyfriend. She got pregnant with Minuit and realised that she could never live with that guy, with any of our fathers. She didn't say anything, he was the one who left. We started our life again by ourselves, the four of us. She didn't recognise you at first, but then yes, if only just. And you, no, you didn't recognise her. That annoyed her, she felt even more alone and isolated.

Actually, she hates you. Well, I don't really know.

232

But, hey, I mean, that's no excuse, I know, I'm sorry, I didn't think about it, about all the shit that's going to hit the fan. That stuff so doesn't matter to me, I mean, I couldn't give a fuck about it, about those sort of things. I'm sorry, Adèle.

He apologises again.

No, you did the right thing.

We just have to tell them not to say anything.

Are you kidding, says Nielle, it's going to get around whether we like it or not.

It doesn't matter, I mean it, I say. It gets me out of having to talk about it, it's all fine.

I know exactly how the rumour will take over the whole countryside: like the thawing of the snow, it's going to be dirty. But it'll be good, it'll be true, it'll be very down-to-earth, one piece of ground after another, step by step.

The whole countryside will be striped in bands of green and grey-white. The whole countryside will be filthy and the plateau will look like what it is: harsh, muddy.

The rumour will travel across the plateau slowly. When the milder weather arrives, the heavy mists, like steaming avalanches, will roll down over the walls of the gorges and it will feel exactly like we're in a bad film. One of those films in which the cinematographer overdoes the lighting.

Months later, the rumour will still be gaining ground. It will take a few weeks before Tony hears about it in the café, or at one of the livestock markets.

~

He'll tell me how he was humiliated in among the animals. He'll tell me about the sarcastic comments in the middle of all the noise, the smell of manure and cigarettes, the whole atmosphere of men in boots, spouting insults, the bulging bellies, the hands in pockets, and the screaming, on top of that, you can't imagine what it was like, the calves screaming, and the others laughing. I was humiliated.

He'll tell me all that while I try to remember vaguely how, by opening the door of the cave, not even two months ago, he brought in the daylight and took me in his fireman's arms, and even cried, out of sight of the others.

I will decide to stay here, because it's my home.

I know time will pass and the gossip, the wounds, will be forgotten. The rumours will become what they were apparently hiding: some sort of truth, mine. I was a boy from here, and I never became a man. I was a boy, and I became a woman from here. I know the plateau is big enough for the tongues to grow weary.

Sylvain is right, they're not all fascists around here. I will have the support of his mother the witch, and of other families, not necessarily those you'd expect.

My brother will come up to support me. It will be undreamed of, instinctive. He'll do the round of the bistros talking about his broken knucklebone and his sister, Adèle. People will pat him on the shoulder, and that will almost be enough to give me back my place back among the locals.

There'll be a few jokes. When they dare to make them in front of me, I'll go one better, and as my porno vocabulary is rich and varied, no one will be able to take it further. So, stupidly, quite simply, it'll be respect.

In the end, it will be me who decides to leave Tony. He will be gobsmacked, agitated, horrible.

He will slap me because I will have smiled and even laughed, laughed far too much at his exasperated gestures. He will try to imitate the men at the livestock market, in order to make me realise how hard it was for him. The most shameful moment of my life. You made me suffer the most shameful moment of my life.

But too bad, I won't be able to stop laughing, because even though I will know how serious it'll be for him, how hurt and beside himself he'll be, it will still be hilarious, and he'll be too stupid, and, anyway, what have I got to lose.

I will laugh like a drain and he will slap me and call me thoughtless, a monster, a kid, an adolescent. You're no better than the little idiots you cart around.

Nielle and Sylvain are on either side of me; they're not talking anymore. I hold back my tears for a bit longer.

And then it passes, it disappears into the charcoal flickerings of the old beech trees.

We stay there for a long time, we stay there all night, my Loire kids and I, our faces red, keeping watch over the others, stoking the fire, without saying anything more, only words without speech, words with gestures, like, leave that, Adèle, I'll do it, when I get up to grab another log.

Nielle stands up straight, his arms full of wood, an exaggerated victory grin on his face. Then he places a log on the embers, pressing down a bit, digging in the crackling ashes as if he wanted to scratch out an extra space in the hearth. He gets up again and rubs his hands, still with the same triumphant expression.

He takes a photograph out of his cloth skirt and tells us that it was hanging on the sign, there, behind the woodpile. It's a photo of the last caretaker to have lived here, until 1928.

In the glow of the fire, the face of the guy from the road appears.

Well, yeah, I dunno, that must be his father, or his grandfather.

So there you go, I say, it's the night of revelations.

And we return to our cosy silence until the early morning, until Tony disturbs us by letting in the daylight, the cold, and noise.

Thank you:

To Lola first of all, who gave this novel a gentle start with her little poem.

To Danielle, and to all the girls born in the body of a boy.

To her brother Stéphan.

To all the children and adolescents who take, have taken or will take the school bus, in particular to Lola, again, and to Paul, Sylvère, Hugo and Jasmin. To all the little wolf pups of the plateaus.

To the men and women bus drivers in the mountains, and to all the snow-plough drivers— nightshift and dayshift.

To those who live in the Vercors region, to Stéphane the rope worker, to everyone from the hamlets of Truc, Bard et des Mondins, to Michel for his letter to the magistrate, and to the people from Greenpeace.

To the *padgels*, everyone living up on the Ardèche plateau, recently arrived or not, to those from the hamlets of La Tauleigne, Verden and those from La Rajasse, and especially to Christian, and to his wolf pups.

To the teachers in the primary and secondary schools in the Vercors Sud and the Haute Ardèche, to Daniel (of the blue cows and the *deux-chevaux*), to Marie-Paule, to Mallaury. To Monique, who was the teacher in the hamlet of Bertoire, even if in this instance I'm fudging the altitude.

To the parents of the students, especially Stéphane.

To the environment officers of Lake Issarlès.

To Jean-Philippe's potato beetle.

It's not a thankyou, but this novel also emerged from the memory of Misty, of her pain and of her mystery.